DEAR TEACHER

A NOVEL

MADDALENA VAGLIO TANET

TRANSLATED FROM THE ITALIAN
BY JILL FOULSTON

HARPERVIA

An Imprint of HarperCollins*Publishers*

This is a work of fiction. Names, characters, places, and incidents are products of the author's imagination or are used fictitiously and are not to be construed as real. Any resemblance to actual events, locales, organizations, or persons, living or dead, is entirely coincidental.

HarperCollins books may be purchased for educational, business, or sales promotional use. For information, please email the Special Markets Department at SPsales@harpercollins.com.

Originally published as *Tornare dal bosco* in Italy in 2023 by Marsilio Editori.

FIRST EDITION

Designed by Tetragon, London

Library of Congress Cataloging-in-Publication Data has been applied for.

ISBN 978-0-06-333917-0

25 26 27 28 29 LBC 5 4 3 2 1

In memory of Ada Maurizio, my grandmother,
Maria Vadori, my great-grandmother,
and Lidia Julio, the teacher

For Paola Savio, my mother

Stones taut in the woods; they have small
friends, ants and other animals
I don't recognize. The wind
doesn't blow away the tombstone, graves, the
shadowy remains, that life of heavy
dreams
You remain in shadow: my heart burns
and then crumbles in order to remember naïvely
not to die.
My heart is like that forest: wholly
sarcastic at times, its filthy branches
falling on your head, burdening you.

AMELIA ROSSELLI, *Documento*

Like eyes these dull holes in the window
on the right the ivy has stripped everything and it seems
beautiful you might say a triumph this greenery
while overhead a bird squawks you see it fly
in circles like someone who speaks to ghosts
what a strange machine, the head, we harass the dead
with our thoughts, caw, caw, it's only a crow.

AZZURRA D'AGOSTINO, *Canti di un luogo abbandonato*

I

INSTEAD OF GOING TO SCHOOL, the teacher went into the woods.

In one hand she held the newspaper she'd just bought and in the other her leather satchel containing notebooks, corrected homework, pens, and well-sharpened pencils. She left the road unhesitatingly, as if the woods had been her destination from the start. Her loafers padded over a carpet of shiny brown leaves that looked like raw entrails.

She soon abandoned the satchel and the newspaper; at a certain point, her grip had loosened without her noticing. She followed one path for a bit, perhaps from muscle memory, and then left it and began ascending and descending the slopes. She felt she was going at great speed, and that the landscape was melting around her. Chestnuts, hazelnut trees, and birches were splotches, rivulets of color; the sky spilled over the outlines of the hills; the earth danced under her feet like a floating jetty.

The percussion of her feet on the level ground became a kind of drumbeat, urging her to continue. She heard the impact, but as if it were coming from underground; someone down there was knocking, forcing her to go on, chasing her away.

After many hours, tiredness compelled her to slow down. She was stumbling, her lips were sticky with saliva and she kept swallowing in an effort to get something down: it felt like she'd swallowed a bite that had become stuck in her throat, but it was her heart, tired out by the march. Her skirt was streaked with mud, her tights shredded by brambles.

The daylight was fading, by this time almost azure, blue. A half-moon materialized above the mountaintops. The teacher recognized the feeling of the cold night air, and it was that familiar sensation which restored a moment of clarity and allowed her to truly suffer.

She had climbed a hill called the Rovella, and from there she could see the village of Bioglio where she'd been born: the roof of the church, its bell tower, the lights going on one by one in the dusk. She saw them, but she couldn't understand them. They seemed like the ruins of a forgotten civilization. She had gotten all the way up there without meaning to, urged on like a blindfolded prisoner. Her stomach was twisting with hunger, the backs of her shoes had rubbed her heels, and even her face hurt because she hadn't stopped clenching her teeth and jaw the entire time. She couldn't go down to her village, nor could she turn around: the hazy memory of her house and the people she knew terrified her.

She wasn't afraid of the woods, though. She'd grown up during a time when they were used like fields and pastures. She'd been going there with her cousin from the time she was a girl, at night, too, to look for mushrooms. They'd gone out alone in the dark, pitch-black, climbing up the shortest, steepest road behind a clutch of houses clinging to the hill. They had a lamp and two sticks for holding back the shrubs and tapping at piles of leaves, a wicker basket with a handle for their treasures. The scent of mold was strong, and they knew how to follow the rot snaking between tufts of grass to find the wild mushrooms. Some of the enormous porcini made them swear for joy. The rest of the time they communicated by nodding and elbowing each other, holding hands only in exceptional cases (a badger too close, a painful slide on the backside, a sprain). They knew every twist in the path, the exposed roots, the eroded earth, the roe deer's tracks and glades where they stopped to sleep, the abandoned dens of foxes, trunks gnawed by dormice. An ash-colored dawn arrived with a timid glow, making the treetops seem even blacker. They'd go there to collect chestnuts, too, cracking the burrs under their little boots.

It was October now. There were mushrooms, hidden, and chestnuts on the ground, but it was 1970 and she was forty-two years old.

The teacher turned her back on the village. She was trembling from head to toe, and within her chest she felt the flapping of wings in the branches like palpitations. She had a flickering memory of an abandoned cabin, an old shelter for animals and tools, its roof in a sorry state. She'd just have to drag herself to the top of the hill where the woods had overtaken the paths and bushes and the sweet acacias had suffocated the other trees. She grabbed at the heather to get back up the incline, directing her feet toward the crags.

The roof of the cabin had been cobbled together a few years before with prefabricated tiling, but since then no one had had the time or strength to keep back the vegetation. There were no stairs to get to the wooden loft and the branches of an acacia were poking through the tiny window. There was still straw on the ground, not all of it moldered, and in one corner old bill-hooks, rakes, and sickles.

The teacher staggered on, paying attention to nothing. She was dazed, and her eyes were seeing things that had nothing to do with where she actually was. As soon as she crossed the threshold she fell to the floor and stopped moving.

2

THAT MORNING she'd gotten up wearily, as always. Her alarm clock sat on a small saucer, and she'd placed coins in it so that whenever the alarm went off, clanging and vibrating, the intolerable sound made her jump. She'd turn it off with a slap, eyes still shut; its many tumbles to the floor had dinged and dented it into something unrecognizable.

The teacher would get up and light the burner under her waiting coffeepot. *Only after a coffee*, she told herself, *will I be able to think.* She'd leave the small empty cup on the table in the midst of the circular prints made by other cups, other coffees drunk over the preceding days.

She'd take off her nightgown in the bathroom and wash her arms and chest, making sure not to neglect any part of her skin because she knew she was careless, and every now and then her cousin's wife would alert her: "Silvia, you should change your jumper. You'll sweat now that the heating is on." She must have smelled of sweat. She didn't notice it, but she didn't want to upset anyone, especially the children. With children you had to be neat and clean because they were forced to be well groomed, and if they were found to have a sweaty collar or dirty nails they got shouted at. So she had gotten into the habit of washing with too much soap. Every week she used entire bars of Felce Azzurra and doused her armpits, underwear, and inside her shoes with talcum powder. But she remained at one with the countryside, the rake and the beasts, and she knew that one day when she retired she would go back to her village and throw fistfuls of salt over red snails to dissolve them before they could attack her lettuces. She'd sweep up hens' droppings, repair the rabbit hutch, and force herself to remember to wash her hands before she ate.

Outside the sky was clear and the light threw the hillside, trees, and buildings into sharp silhouette. At least two people saw her walking down the road that slithered around the incline: Signora Berti, from a window in her house between two medlar trees, and then Giulio Motta, who was having coffee on his balcony with the cat on his knees.

Everyone in the neighborhood knew the teacher. She had moved to Biella as a young girl for school, and she hadn't gone anywhere since then aside from a few coach trips to Valle d'Aosta and Switzerland, and to Liguria to dip her toes in the water. She'd taken her one flight to visit relatives in Melbourne, Australia, but she remembered almost nothing of that trip, saying only, "It was nice," or "If they see a kangaroo, they run over it or put it on the barbecue." And if someone pressed her on that—"What do you mean, Silvia? How do they manage to hit them?" or "Poor things," "But isn't the car damaged?"—she just shrugged. She often shrugged, was often lost in thought, and she walked with her head down, lower lip protruding, brow furrowed. She looked at her feet or at the road ahead of her and her close-set blue eyes remained hidden beneath their lids.

She lived on the edge of the city, where multi-story blocks of flats with lifts alternated with houses and their gardens, wild meadows, kitchen gardens, and chicken coops. Sorb hedges thrust clusters of orange berries out onto the pavements, and even at that early hour piles of dead branches and foliage left after pruning were already burning in courtyards. The smoke hit her sideways, in gusts, while the stench of rotten foliage rose from gutters and ditches. She inhaled deeply and thought that some pungent odors were, after all, agreeable. She liked the smell of cellars and the skin of salami, for example. On the other hand, she hated the smell of milk simmering on the cooker, which she blamed on her years at boarding school, when they gave her sour milk at breakfast, lunch, and dinner.

She would hurriedly buy a paper from the newsagent at the bottom of the hill because she wanted to get to class early and finish writing out the homework she'd assigned to her students. She made each child a copy by hand in her clear, neat writing.

Signor Minero in the newsagents didn't dare say anything and he didn't stop her. Anyway, he wasn't sure whether the girl was one of her students. Perhaps Silvia barely knew her. Mainly, he was embarrassed: he didn't want to be the first to talk to her about it. Clearly, he would have been the first—almost no one knew, it was still early, and she seemed wholly unaware of what had happened. And what if she started crying? Or fell to the ground?

While he was mentally trying out a few phrases (*Silvia, did you see? Silvia, have you heard? Silvia, wait*), clearing his voice and opening his mouth to speak, she went out. She left some coins, the right amount, on the plastic tray and was instantly out of the door.

"Didn't she even read the headlines?" he was asked later.

"No, she folded the paper in half, shoved it in her handbag, and left."

Who can say whether it would have made any difference if she had discovered what had happened to the girl while she was not alone? She might have collapsed right there in front of them. She wouldn't have been able to leave like that, on her own, as if nothing had happened. Minero would have taken her home or phoned her relatives: *Something's happened—come and get Silvia.* Or maybe she would have trembled, hesitated, then pulled herself together, gripped her handbag, and said, *I'm all right. I'll go to school anyway.* Instead she had gone into the woods.

"I should have stopped her," Minero repeated over the following days.

"That ass, Minero! Why didn't he stop her?" thundered Silvia's cousin, the closest relative she had. He was over six feet tall, and his voice shook the glasses.

"Don't shout, Anselmo." His wife tried to calm him, unable to bear her husband's fussing, his theatrical eruptions.

"He's a prat! I've always said so!" he went on, shouting like crazy and beating the table with hands as large as spades.

"That's enough. You'll have a seizure."

"Idiot!"

"Oh come on! Why do you care about Minero? We should focus on Silvia. Where might she have gone? Where could she have slipped and fallen?"

"Quiet, you. You don't understand a thing," Anselmo shouted, and he clenched his fists to squeeze out his anguish.

3

THE TWO-STORY SCHOOL BUILDING was the color of milky coffee and surrounded by a narrow mesh fence, hydrangeas, and cherry laurel. The playground was paved over in gravel and cement with insets for grass where little trees were growing, tormented by the youngest children who climbed on them and tore off their leaves to make "soup." It was a fifteen-minute walk from the newsagents.

"She must have opened the paper on the way," they later surmised.

In fact, the teacher had taken the paper from her handbag while she was still walking. She liked to scan the headlines at least before getting to school, to feel more firmly attached to the world. *You've got your head in the clouds, Silvia. You're off with the fairies.* People always said that. She shook the paper open and at that moment, by the side of the road, she read the news. She stopped abruptly, seemingly unperturbed, and yet, if one had looked closer, her stillness might have appeared unnatural. There was an avalanche inside her. Almost immediately, she was unable to decipher the characters, but in the rubble of letters a few isolated words continued to pulsate before her eyes: *fell, body, tragedy*. After a minute or so, she turned the page to find the end of the article and a photo of the large block of flats with a torrent, the Cervo, winding below it.

She became aware that she was walking again, her legs carrying her miraculously and without her intervention. She hurried along, like someone late for an appointment, and only now and then did she stumble or her ankle give way. But she couldn't have said whether she was limping or her shoulder was hurting; she'd brushed against a wall (plaster dust had left a clear mark on her raincoat, or maybe it was chalk from the blackboard the day before). She passed the hospital and let herself be led down the hill. The pavement beside the cement wall was narrow, and the passing cars rattled and shook over the cobblestones.

At the last bend in the road the Cervo and the bridge came into sight, and she realized that her legs were dying to throw her into the water. She had nothing against this plan. It didn't matter to her, and actually it seemed reasonable, even logical. It would be easy to get over the railing: no one paid her any attention, and no one would get there in time to stop her. But, to her surprise, she covered the entire span and reached the opposite bank as if she were cycling, and in fact she felt a cramp in her stomach because she wasn't far from the block of flats shown in the paper, and she remembered, momentarily, the tale of the Pied Piper who drowns rats in the river and then drowns the children, too, in revenge. She was the rat, but the sequence was all wrong: the rat comes before the girl, not after.

She'd missed her chance and had to go on; she thought she'd

probably walk until she fainted and that, too, would be fine with her, though it would take a lot longer.

Her eyesight worsened; she no longer recognized shapes. It felt like the woods had come after her, entangling her in a jumble of trunks, spines, and foliage.

4

SHE WAS NEVER LATE, so everyone was alarmed by her absence. The news, meanwhile, had arrived at the school as well. The police inspector asked for a meeting with the headmaster and teachers as soon as lessons were finished. A couple of journalists started taking photos of the building just as the children swarmed through the gate. One second-year pupil called out a greeting: "Ciao, Uncle!"

It was a small town.

There was an empty desk in class now, and Silvia was nowhere to be seen. They figured she must have found out—someone must have called her, a journalist or a relative up early—and that she hadn't felt like leaving the house. It was another teacher, Sister Annangela, one of her closest friends, who phoned her apartment. When she got no response she phoned Silvia's cousin Anselmo, only two doors away. His mother-in-law answered.

"Good morning, Gemma, it's Sister Annangela."

"How are you? Is everything okay?"

"Can't complain, Gemma, can't complain. I'm looking for Silvia—is she at your place? I understand if she doesn't feel like coming in today . . ."

"She's not here."

"Oh," said Sister Annangela, before repeating, "She's not with you." The headmaster in front of her shook his head as if it were mounted on a spring, and another teacher, Fogli, sniffed.

"But what's wrong, Sister Annangela?"

"Maybe she's at home but isn't picking up her phone. That could be it. Would you mind checking?"

"Sure. I've got the keys. But you're worrying me."

"Well, Gemma, it concerns a student, a girl in year six, Silvia's class." Sister Annangela's voice broke despite her efforts. "She's gone. She passed away last night."

"Oh, Madonna. Oh, my God." Gemma held the receiver away from her ear and looked at it as if it were guilty. "How could she have known?"

"Someone may have phoned her early this morning, or maybe she bought the paper, read the news, and went back home."

"An accident?" Gemma asked.

"In the Cervo, in the river. We don't know anything for sure."

"Poor dear. May the Lord take her to glory," Gemma said. She was very devout and whenever she turned to God her Friulian accent took over.

"I know, it's dreadful. A child. Eleven years old. We're shocked. If she's heard about it, Silvia, too, must be upset. It was one of her students. She really looked after her. Go and check, Gemma."

"I'll call you back, Sister Annangela."

Gemma put down the phone and left the house, her apron still tied and her shoes only half on.

"They'll call back," Annangela said to the head. "I'm going to look in on the class."

Her heart sank, for the girl and now also for Silvia. She knew her, knew she wouldn't be able to bear up under the sorrow. She might seem solid and opaque, like a slab of ice you could walk on without worrying about it cracking. But in fact the ice was thin, a barely thickened membrane.

She went into the year-six class, which was waiting and being looked after by a caretaker with a somber expression. The students still knew nothing.

Sister Annangela was very short and stout, with feet so small they looked round and calves like two sausages stuffed into the thick brown tights that nuns wore.

"Be patient, children. Your teacher, Canepa, may have been taken ill. We're trying to find out." She signaled to a girl sitting in the front row. "Excuse me, I don't know your surname."

"Cairoli."

"Right, Cairoli. Please hand me your textbook."

She put on her glasses, ran her stubby finger over the table of contents, and assigned some reading: *The Elephant's Child.*

"Read the text silently and underline nouns in red, verbs in blue, and adjectives in yellow."

She gave the caretaker a consoling look and went back to her class of second years, small children beaming with unexpected freedom. There, too, a caretaker was monitoring the chatter. One student stood in front of the perfectly clean blackboard with the air of someone who'd had a prickly chestnut burr slipped into his pants.

"What are you doing there, Martinelli?"

"I sent him there, Sister Annangela, because he said something dirty about your absence."

Sister Annangela felt a smile breaking out and she pressed her lips together hoping to suppress it, at least partially.

"Crikey! Something dirty. Something I have to hear."

She didn't want to embarrass the caretaker by revoking the punishment, but neither did she want to leave the child standing there. Not that day.

"Not that dirty, Sister Annangela," Martinelli protested.

"He said . . ." The caretaker looked for the right paraphrase. "He said you were in the loo, Sister Annangela."

"Interesting."

"Doing your business."

"I get it. Thank you."

"Sorry!" the boy blurted out, on the verge of tears.

They take everything terribly seriously, Sister Annangela thought, struck by a wave of sadness. Marina Poggio was scratching inside her ear with the rubber on her pencil. Ludovico Bindi balanced on his knees the apple he would eat during break. Sister Annangela herself tasted salty tears in her throat.

"You're excused, Martinelli. Go back to your seat. And anyway, for your information, I wasn't in the loo."

She sat down, and for a moment she feared she wouldn't be able to face the morning or the days to come. The funeral. She hung her head. The children looked at her. "Crikey," she said again, and their eyes widened like those of a row of little owls. She'd have to move them into the other second-year classroom and go back to the girl's class, where they were still reading *The Elephant's Child*, completely oblivious. They had no idea.

5

GEMMA RANG THE BELL and knocked again and again without an answer. She put her ear to the shutter but heard no noise. Then, steadying her hand, she opened the door to Silvia's house.

She was used to emergencies. She knew the tension that lashes the body like a steel cable. She was from Friuli, where she'd been born in 1903. Whenever anyone talked about the Second World War she'd say, "Just think: I've been through two of them." She enjoyed saying that. She enjoyed the fact that she was still alive despite the Battle of Caporetto, the Spanish flu, widowhood, bombs, and the German roundups, though many people she knew felt guilt more than anything else. Her daughter, Luisa, for a start. But for Gemma the past was just that: it was behind her, gone. *I won't end up fleeing at night, I won't get across the bridge by a whisker before it blows up, my daughter won't be sent to Germany to work like a slave.* She maintained that this was all anyone needed in order to live optimistically.

Yet that morning, when she found Silvia's house empty, Gemma was overcome with an inexplicable sense of danger. It was too early to become alarmed. Silvia couldn't have left much more than an hour ago: the coffee grounds in her cup were still wet, her bed was unmade, the soap had slid onto the green tiles of the bathroom floor. The teacher wasn't your typical housekeeper, so nothing strange about that. But as for being there: she wasn't. Gemma promptly phoned the school to let them know.

6

WHILE SHE'S SLEEPING, something rips open her stomach. She is the one doing it. She scrapes away the pulp with a knife, as if peeling a medlar until only the shiny kernel is left, a strange contrast with the fruit. She sees it glowing like a little black sun, a rejected black egg. A hollow Easter egg, nothing inside.

The teacher opens her eyes. As soon as she closes them the images appear. The ribs of a calf, a mole drowned for tunneling through the kitchen garden, billhooks on the cellar wall, a frog's pulsing throat, which you can puncture with a needle or chop off: you draw a line with a knife, the way you would underline a word or cross it out to correct it. She sees mountains of notebooks with all the words crossed out, a dusty classroom, but maybe the particles in the air are ashes, and she finds herself in an empty fireplace—enormous like the one in Verrès Castle, which she has visited many times with her classes. Yet no, that can't be, because her grandmother is dragging her feet around the room there. Silvia hears the rustling of her slippers and petticoat. A man carries a pheasant over his shoulders, head dangling, eye cloudy. An obese woman heads toward the loo at the back of the courtyard, looks around, and pulls up her skirt; because of her bulk, she can't get all the way into the poky room and part of her is forced to remain outside. Trembling with the effort not to topple over, she grabs the frame of the gaping door. She doesn't know that a few young boys are climbing up on the pergola to steal grapes, and now, laughing, they watch her from above. She doesn't know it, but Silvia hears their muffled cackling.

The more violent her visions, the more they calm rather than scare her. Not far away, boars grumble. A blackcap whistles; it must be nearly morning. She doesn't formulate this thought, but her ears register the sound and inside her something answers: blackcap. It's a reflection more than information and is soon forgotten. Her senses bring her material, her brain tries to function, but it's all a black sludge of indifference.

Through the door of the hut Silvia makes out a birch tree with its fruit. The image slams into her and she is tempted to use her arms to shield herself. The fruit of the birch look like little brown salamis dangling there. They crumble into powder on first contact, releasing their seeds. Anything that droops, leans, or hangs from a hook is fine by her. She herself feels like that, a bundle hanging by the waist from a skinny stem, which might also be a noose. Above her head the crooked roof reveals patches of the sky, growing ever brighter.

Outside is a beech whose bark has been colonized by bracket fungus: dozens of ash-gray hats protrude from the trunk like hoofs. The bark is already flaking off; large slabs of it are missing. Silvia knows there's no escape for the tree: sooner or later it will fall. She knows this, but nothing is organizing itself in a coherent whole, into before and after, and anyway she doesn't see any great difference between herself and plants with their parasites, mold on planks, living animals and their carcasses, the breeze coming through the door and cracks. She needs to urinate but doesn't see why she should get up, go outside, and do that like the fat woman mocked by the boys' excited gaze. She empties her bladder right where she is, not moving an inch.

7

GIOVANNA: THAT WAS THE GIRL'S NAME. At the end of the previous year she'd started skipping class. She'd never done very well at school; she was slow.

"What's this all about? You can't afford to stay at home," Silvia told her. She kept her back after class and did her homework with her. She sat beside her, ill at ease yet determined, meanwhile unwrapping the sandwiches she'd prepared for the two of them. They were the only thing Silvia made in her kitchen other than coffee, since she always ate supper with Anselmo and Luisa. Mostly she put slices of cheese in those sandwiches, because she'd noticed Giovanna preferred that, or butter and jam.

"Everyone gets better with practice. Look at me. I'm not that bright, but I made an effort." She said it without false modesty. It was the truth, and it had to be faced; she wouldn't take compliments. Silvia felt she was at least intelligent enough to know that she wasn't a genius. A completely normal brain, a dash of perseverance, diligence. At boarding school, where she'd studied after the war, the good ones were the others, girls who learned without trying, knew things instinctively or made them up. But not her; she did what she had to. She had a sense of duty and determination, an awareness of being too awkward and insecure to carry the weight of being considered a dunce. As an orphan, she'd grown up with her grandparents, and ended up in boarding school. She couldn't bear being told off or humiliated because of her performance at school.

"Come on, Giovanna, let's do your homework together. That way you'll be set for tomorrow."

"Thanks, Miss," the girl replied. And then she was quiet because her mouth was full.

Giovanna's parents were herders who had moved to Biella a few years before. Her mother shuttled back and forth from the shepherd's cottage in the Elvo Valley, where her sister and brother-in-law still lived. Their children went to school in the village of Bagneri. There was only one class and desks and benches were pushed together to form a single block of dark wood, like the pews in church. Giovanna, too, had started elementary school there, but in December she'd caught pneumonia, was admitted to the hospital, and missed nearly three months of school. When she'd stepped back into her classroom, still exhausted and having lost weight, she didn't remember any of the standard Italian her teacher had taught her.

That same year her father had found work in a textile factory, an industry that had exploded after the war and was still growing. He didn't like it but he had a decent salary, his children could go to school in town, and they had an indoor loo, even a bath and a washing machine. The washing machine was a secondhand Candy Superautomatic 5, barely dented by the hail that had fallen on it during delivery.

All over, people were leaving their villages and valleys and Giovanna's father left, too, but he was unhappy and embittered. Like everyone else, he drank and held it well: a bottle a day was nothing for him. Yet every now and then he overdid it, added a little grappa or ratafia. He missed the haystacks, the rattling of the dog's chain at night, cows with their long eyelashes, even the steaming manure on frozen, trampled grass. He inflicted his dissatisfaction on others. He groped his wife roughly in bed and wouldn't stop even when she complained or the children in the next room mumbled in their sleep. Giovanna had failed at school and started over in year one, but she continued to get poor marks. Her father's method of discipline was to hit her, never systematically, never for long. But his calloused hands left bruises that took weeks to fade.

Giovanna was fed up with being hit and she tried hard to make a good impression on her new teacher in town. With great effort on both sides she got a pass mark, but once left to herself she'd started to sink. She'd been about to fail the third year but Silvia hadn't felt like handing her over to another teacher so she'd pulled her along with her, raising Giovanna's marks for drawing, PE, and crafts.

Something changed at the end of her fourth year. The girl became cheeky but also more sensitive. At times her eyes blazed with bewilderment: she'd started growing body hair and her breasts were developing. She used her fingers to hide the mustache sprouting under her nose; when she saw it in direct light from the bulb over the bathroom mirror, it reminded her of the film of mold staining the corners of the ceiling gray.

Although she feared Giovanna's father's reaction, Silvia had not managed to prevent her getting a string of low marks. "Two more smacks, Miss," Giovanna commented laconically.

The family lived in a large council block called the Big House, which loomed over the Cervo between factories that had used hydraulic energy to wash wool for a century and a half. Concrete pillars and cement castings alternated with redbrick arches and the smokestacks of eighteenth-century mills.

The Big House was teeming with children and teenagers and some of the boys had begun to stare at Giovanna, which made her feel dirty but important. She didn't know whether to strut her stuff or run away. Two of them, Michele and Domenico, didn't only look and whistle; they spoke to her in dialect, acting tough as if they were already grown men. Like Giovanna's, their bodies manifested the inconsistencies of puberty. She had two little mounds sticking straight out of her chest, seemingly ready to puncture her T-shirt, and two tufts under her armpits, but her behind was still flat and her hips were barely outlined under a child's egg-shaped tummy. They had enormous hands planted at the end of fidgety arms, Adam's apples like nuts caught in their throats, a few sparse whiskers on their chins but hopelessly smooth necks and cheeks.

At first, Giovanna didn't answer them. She was stupefied with embarrassment, and her field of vision shrank to a square floating in front of her feet as she tried to avoid them, turning at the first possible corner and taking the stairs two at a time so she could disappear. As soon as she was beyond their reach she felt herself buzzing with nervousness and her heart pounded—yet it made her afternoons more exciting, and the following day she'd offer to go and ask a neighbor for some washing powder or stand on the landing for no reason, hazard a trip to the courtyard where she walked up and down, head bowed, pretending she'd lost something just to see if those two would talk to her.

Silvia sensed the significance of the change but couldn't keep up with it. A spinster nearing old age, she was treated as a nun by all. Whenever she thought about herself she imagined a plantlike organism, a body less chaste than indifferent. She tried to scold the child. "You're distracted! I can't do everything for you myself. Come on, so we can finish quickly. Pay attention, or I'll have to give you a really low mark. Giovanna, you're not listening to me."

It wasn't that Giovanna had lost her fear of beatings; what's more, her mother had begun to turn against her too. To hear her, you'd think her daughter was in constant danger. Now that she was growing up, there was a lot at stake. Her mother thought of her precocious development as bad luck. Having breasts at eleven years old was a misfortune, exposing her to dangers she didn't want to deal with, worn out as she was by her bothersome husband, going back and forth to the Alpine hut, and her younger children, who used the umbrella ribs like spears to poke holes in the furniture. She convinced Giovanna that her boobs were a couple of bombs about to explode.

Giovanna couldn't stand people talking about her body. It sent her into a rage. She no longer recognized herself, and as she struggled to make sense of it, the fact that everyone else was talking about the ongoing changes made her feel exposed, caught out. She wished for darkness, silence. The word "breast" in her mother's mouth made her gag, made her seem smutty and prying. She was seething with anger and talked back rudely so her mother threatened to have her father punish her, and then Giovanna would leave, banging the door.

She seemed to haunt her own body. Little Giovanna had been decanted into the body of a misshapen young woman, a stranger.

In the Elvo Valley where she'd been born was a woman who worked as a medium. Behind her back she was called *la masca*, the witch: ghosts would enter her and move her arms and hands; their voices came rasping from her throat. People went to her to learn where a dead person had hidden their money, whether they'd been faithful, if they were vengeful. *La masca* didn't seem all that happy about acting as the puppet for the dead, but the money, plump rabbits, and full jugs of wine suited her. Giovanna remembered her because she, too, had to inhabit a strange body, like the spirits swirling around the living body of the witch. And this was ongoing, not just for five minutes.

On the other hand, in a strange way it made her stronger. An arrow seemed to point at her wherever she went and, little by little, her aversion to the looks skimming over her was blended with a degree of curiosity. It was no longer a big deal: she was still just a little girl, and nobody thought about going further. Yet she sensed this was only the beginning, the trigger for something that would let her get away from her violent father, her distracted mother. She started reading photoromances published by Lancio, packed with heroines both poor and romantic: Letizia, Marina, Charme. She dreamed of having a crocheted cotton purse and long stockings instead of knee socks. And though she hated her face and little mustache, she daydreamed about receiving a love letter.

She'd ended up making friends with the two boys from the Big House. It was a relationship in which physical proximity failed to become intimacy. They spent time together in the same place, usually the courtyard or the boulders beside the stream, so they were friends and signaled that to the world, particularly to the other kids in the council block. But they never touched, not even by mistake or to help each other up and down the steep slopes between boulders. At most, they splashed each other with icy water, which was sometimes very clean and other times spotted with yellow and brown foam from the woolen mills.

Giovanna felt she didn't know much about them and they knew nothing about her. When she went back home, it was as if she'd changed her skin yet again. But they would talk. About the rich kids in Michele and Domenico's class, for example, and how they played dirty in the football matches that took place in the courtyard. About the moon landing. About Lele, the disabled boy who lived on the first floor and was always in his pajamas and wore handkerchiefs around his neck like a cowboy to catch his drooling. About the old man who'd lurk in the park to show his thing to people who were pissing in the bushes. About their parents, who tried to keep them under control. Not wanting to be outdone, Giovanna said that her teacher would do better to find herself a boyfriend instead of breathing down her neck, but when the other two said, "Who'd want that old hag?" she immediately came to her defense. "But you've never seen her.

She's not that bad. Pretty old, for sure, but not that bad. She's a pain in the arse, though," she added, not looking at them.

At a certain point they started skipping school. Walking around instead of sitting at their desks—it felt intoxicating. Domenico and Michele smoked noxious cigarettes. Giovanna wished she could ring all the intercoms and go looking for tadpoles, but instead she ended up hanging around the boys, imitating the laughter of uninhibited women—the usual photoromance heroines, but also Romy Schneider and, closer to home, Vanda from the haberdashery, who'd touch up her red lipstick in front of clients, and also Marilisa, the older sister of one of her classmates. In order to convince herself that growing up was exciting, Giovanna overdid it, flaunting herself in a sort of caricature. Obviously they were spotted, and obviously her father found out about it and beat her. Her teacher tried to avoid giving her bad grades so as not to aggravate the situation.

Giovanna felt like someone had tricked her. She hadn't started growing up on purpose. She tried not to lose her balance as she was dragged along, and if she tripped up it wasn't her fault. One day she would put a cigarette stub in her mouth, another she'd meekly follow the teacher's lessons. She'd lock herself in the bathroom, grit her teeth, and rip the hair from her calves with duct tape, or she'd take her mother's mirror to find out at last what she had between her thighs. Then she'd go out and play desperately with her brothers, completely forgetting her older friends, playing truant, or anatomical matters. She'd start the day proud and daring and finish it subdued and crippled with embarrassment.

There was only one constant: for some months, her father's beatings on her new body had been unbearable, even more so than her mother's probing looks. She couldn't stand being touched other than by her little brothers, who jumped on her back or tugged at her. Many fathers beat their children—she didn't feel singled out or sad. Above all, she was unsure exactly whom her father was beating. So her usual defenses, which on good days had allowed her to feel indifferent, didn't work anymore.

8

GIOVANNA SPENT SUMMERS at her aunt and uncle's Alpine hut. Her father stayed in town because of his work: good riddance. The smell of hay and animals seeped into everything, the sun burned, and the wind bellowed too. Morning and evening, at milking time, her uncle called the cows by name and they showed up one after another like obedient dogs. Their names weren't very imaginative: Chestnut, Red Girl, White Girl, Star, Spotty . . . Chestnut was the queen and she led the others up and down crags and slopes. At the start of the season she was pregnant, so they put her in the paddock with the leader of a neighboring herd and the two planted themselves in front of each other, horn to horn, jostling calmly for hours to see who would be dominant. They didn't go overboard or wound each other, careful not to endanger their unborn calves. Colossa was black, and on her head she had a shock of brown hair.

"Five hundred and sixty kilos of cow!" her owner boasted. But in the end, Chestnut had run her off.

Butter was made straight after the daily milking, and *toma* and *maccagno* cheeses were started. Yellow butter came from the cream in the churn, and Giovanna's aunt would decorate it with a wooden stamp showing scrolls, zigzags, and stylized flowers. Giovanna went at it; sweat stains splotched her dress. She sat on a stool between barrels and basins in the cool preserved by the north-facing stone walls. Her cousin Pietro would glance at her as he passed the doorway, a scythe hanging from his belt. But in the mountains she felt in charge of her own life again and she allowed herself to ignore him. She wrapped her hair in a handkerchief and pushed her fringe back mercilessly, though once freed it would stand up in a tuft on her forehead, making her look ridiculous. Tufted tit, her cousin Flora called her. So what, she was too busy to care. When the butter was ready, she had to heat the skimmed milk in copper cauldrons to make curd. Giovanna helped to pour it into molds and stamp it with designs. Her aunt also made *primo sale* and small *toma* cheeses, which she seasoned with herbs and sold in the co-op along with the butter. It took months, though, for the larger *toma.*

Giovanna's brothers prodded the pig with hazelnut twigs, gave him peelings and leftover polenta or pasta to eat, caressed his soft ear bristles. Uncle never took off his hat or velvet gilet, not even on the hottest days, when all he did was roll up his shirtsleeves and curse the heavens. He'd kick his dog, Turbo, and right afterward order him to come close so he could put a reassuring hand on his black-and-white head. He behaved like that with everyone, whether people or animals.

"Scram! Come here!" A slap, an affectionate pat. You just had to get used to it. It was his version of family intimacy. He and his eldest son didn't know how to talk about things without shouts and insults, but it didn't mean they were angry. It was the only way they knew how to communicate, completely indifferent to the shouting, swearing, palms beating the table. Their ill-humor was a private language with no real meanness at its heart.

At least that's how it seemed to Giovanna, who served their *caffè corretto* in small glasses. Uncle and cousin drank it down in one sip and then went to lie down peacefully. They'd sleep for an hour, wake up disgruntled again, bolt down another coffee. They swore at the hens scratching outside the door, jerking their heads sideways ten, a hundred times, wattles flapping. They went back to work. They had to mow and turn the grass so it would dry and become hay; cut wood; clean the stables; manage the beehives. Their honey tasted of rhododendron and Alpine flowers. They ate it all year round in town, and Giovanna's father would swirl it in his milk with a sense of nostalgia that turned to fury.

Whenever he came up to visit, Giovanna avoided him as much as possible. He seemed to have a devil in him and he criticized everything. At night he'd sit and peer at the open fan of the Alps, looking surly. The mountains would turn purple, then light blue, and finally dark blue. The stars would come out and he'd feel them as pangs in his chest. If his wife tried to come near, he'd chase her away angrily.

"Damn it! I can't have a moment of peace." If he had to hit someone he didn't offer aimless slaps like Uncle's, easy to dodge; he made sure he hit home. Still, no one complained too much. After he'd gone, Giovanna's mother and her aunt would say, "What a temper! What a wretched beast!" but with no bitterness. Hatred, however, often surged in Giovanna. She felt it surface in her stomach like the cream she separated from the milk every day.

She liked her sickle-carrying cousin well enough, but Giovanna had discovered in those summer months that when it came down to it, cheese interested her more than boys. Working made her feel good and she sensed her aunt's approving glances settling on the back of her neck like butterflies on the gentians in the meadow. Once more, her legs were for running and her hands for making things, and their appearance and texture meant nothing. Her aunt had a big wobbly arse and a load of flabby skin around her arm muscles but she was unstoppable, a bulldozer, Uncle said proudly, and while she hoisted her huge behind up the ladder he'd give it two or three vigorous pats.

Flora was jealous because, unlike Giovanna, she didn't yet have her period, and Giovanna treated her like a moron. They'd make peace at night in their shared bed. Under tented sheets, they combed each other's blond hair with their fingers and swore undying affection, talked about when they would have children and it would be their turn to keep them in order with a "Shut up! That's enough. It's time to sleep."

But August was coming to an end; it had been drizzling for days. The time had come to go back to Biella. Her cousins envied Giovanna and her brothers: winter in the village stretched before them, long and sad. And Giovanna envied her cousins: winter in town coursed through the mind like a dirty stream. Her father came to collect her with his customary ill-humor.

Father and daughter were perhaps similar, both wishing they could stay in the mountains and move from the Alps only to the farmstead farther down the mountain. But they wouldn't have guessed this.

At school, Silvia found Giovanna somewhat surly, at war with the world but proud. She convinced herself that Giovanna would pull through by the end of the year, but within a week the girl had fallen into a strange sort of apathy. She'd flick through photoromances behind the lid of her desk, though without much interest. When she skipped school with the two boys from the Big House, instead of feeling excited, she spent those stolen hours in troubled silence, or else she'd passively obstruct all their decisions, as if to rain on their parade. Everything seemed ugly to her. Ugly Michele and Domenico, those two overgrown puppies who'd greeted her return, tails wagging—ugly; the Big House with its gray courtyard and rusty iron gate—ugly; school—ugly; pavement and flowerbeds—ugly; she herself—ugly; her father—super-ugly.

She stared at the short black hairs growing on his nose until he shouted at her to go to hell. At night she'd hear him snoring, her stomach clenched in disgust. Sometimes she wished he'd just die so she could cry at the funeral and others would console her, convince her that she'd loved him. She wished she were good at school, just to amaze him. But more than that, she wanted to make him suffer for once, to make him carry the blame.

9

GIOVANNA DID VERY POORLY in the first assignment of the year. Silvia corrected it, marking the whole thing with red. She didn't know whether to give Giovanna a very low mark or an encouraging one, and she didn't want to use her father's beatings to force her to apply herself—it seemed disloyal. But neither could she treat her differently from the other children. She felt she was losing her authority, and not marking her down would only make matters worse. Unless Giovanna realized that her behavior had consequences she would never shake off her lethargy. In fact, maybe this terrible assignment was a cry for help, and pretending that it wasn't so bad would be tantamount to ignoring her.

In the end, Silvia thought it was the first bad mark she'd given, and that Giovanna could improve. It was better to give it now than later. She marked her just above failure. But she slept badly that night.

Giovanna took back her homework in class without batting an eyelid. When the bell rang, Silvia stopped her.

"You can do better. Don't worry."

"Yes, Miss."

"Is anything wrong?"

"No."

"I saw you out with those guys. Do you want to fail again?"

"No, Miss."

"You've already skipped four days in less than a month of school."

"I was sick one of those days."

"If you miss another day I'll have to tell your parents, you know that? School is a requirement. Let's finish out the year, Giovanna."

The girl nodded and slipped away.

Silvia went home dragging her feet, which seemed heavier with every step, her legs two pig's trotters. She imagined Giovanna going home with her homework in her schoolbag, waiting for her father to return. *What should I have done?* The assignment wasn't salvageable, she said to herself. She thought about calling Giovanna's home, but that seemed excessive. Anyway, how many times had it happened? A poor mark, a few smacks. Almost all her students got them, some more than others. Several of the boys even bragged about them. But it was Giovanna's look that made Silvia uneasy. Her eyes seemed to turn inward.

The next day Giovanna was in class, and it didn't seem that she'd been beaten badly. During break she played with the others and talked nonstop to the girl she sat next to; the daughter of a pharmacist, she did well in school. Silvia felt encouraged. *I'm the one who's making a meal of this*, she said to herself. But within a week Giovanna was skipping school again.

The teacher looked at her empty desk, thinking. *If I phone now, her mother will be at home and she can tell me if Giovanna has a fever or some other setback. I'll phone and convince her to go easy on her. Maybe forbid her to go out in the afternoon, yes, but smacks: no. She's not a dog.*

She phoned. At seven thirty, Giovanna had gone out with her schoolbag as usual and seemed bursting with good health. When she found out about her daughter's absence, Giovanna's mother immediately became agitated.

"That good-for-nothing! When she gets home I'll show her!" She didn't want to let on that she didn't consider school important—she herself had stopped after the third year.

"Oh no, Signora. That's not why I called. I'm worried about Giovanna—recently she seems listless."

"That's because she's hanging out with those two morons."

"I think the best thing to do is to talk to her but without going on the attack. She's at a tricky age. I've been her teacher for over four years and I've never found her to be uncooperative."

"I'm telling you, she's just really stubborn."

"I don't know, I don't know. Will you promise to try and go easy on her? Let's try. Trying doesn't cost a thing."

"Sure, Miss. Thank you for calling."

Giovanna knocked at ten past one and pretended nothing was amiss. Her mother studied her and held back from laying into her right away with the slap that was tickling her right hand. After lunch the girl started washing up without complaining. Conscientiously, she plunged her hands into the soapy water while her brothers played Shanghai. She ran her fingers down the hot ceramic plates until they squeaked to make sure there wasn't any grease left on them.

That afternoon, seeing that she wasn't about to confess, her mother took her aside.

"Your teacher called, so I know you weren't at school. Why are you such a liar?"

Giovanna stood rooted to the spot, saying nothing. A few seconds of silence, broken by the grinding of the washing machine.

"I don't feel like keeping this from your father. I don't want to be a liar like you. But I'll try to keep him calm—your teacher asked me to do that. I'm not sure I'll manage—we both know what he's like. But you're not making it easy. All you have to do is go to school and get a pass. Why do you rile him up like this?"

"If you tell him, I'll kill myself," Giovanna replied, and she went to the children's room and shut the door. Her mother shook her head. She didn't believe it for an instant.

Giovanna, however, opened the window. The river ran past four floors below. The apartment block ended at a stone and cement wall just over the bank, a step away from the gray-green water. Giovanna could make out pebbles on the riverbed, stirred by the Cervo as it smoothed and rounded them like sweets, muddy weeds, a can of paint, a nylon sock. She wasn't thinking about the meadows ready for haymaking, cheese molds, the wind blowing off the glacier, bringing with it the scent of snow even in midsummer, the animals' bluish drooling.

She kicked off her slippers. She seemed to be on the moon, looking down on everything from far away: her house, her family, her father ready to finish his shift and come home, herself at the window. She felt hurt and remote. She wanted to go backward somehow, but also not to go back at all anymore. The only clear thought she had was this: she didn't want to be punished. If anything, she wanted to punish.

They found her three kilometers downstream.

10

GIOVANNA APPEARED TOWARD EVENING. She was a tall girl with a vast repertoire of hostile expressions. To Silvia, she now seems a tiny thing with a long chin, pointy elbows, her shoulder blades little wings, and a dirty-blond fringe bouncing over inhuman eyes. She sits in front of Silvia in the tumbledown hut, her thin wrists protruding from sleeves too short for her like thigh bones on a chicken leg.

All this time, the phone call with Giovanna's mother is going around and around in her head. She tries furiously to change some of what she said, sure that Giovanna's father was told and that it triggered an argument, some punishment.

That's why the girl is dead, and Silvia is her betrayer. She sees the blows: slaps or worse, lashings from a belt that sear her skin. She sees Giovanna crying with blind rage, running to the window, jumping onto the windowsill, and throwing herself out. She hears the thud of her body, still alive, its impact on the boulders, and then the Cervo's immense whirlpools: silent, liquid galaxies. Down there, stippled trout swim between scraps of fabric and tiny fragments of submerged rubbish, coins, so many lost things not made to be in the water, which break down and finally decompose.

She tears herself back—and it's the morning of the previous day.

Silvia recalls going to the phone, looking at the class agenda to find the number, putting her index finger in the hole to dial, rotating the plastic disk four, five, six times. She makes up different versions and an equal number of ways out: she changes her mind, the line is busy, she has the wrong number, Giovanna's mother doesn't answer. The effort of going back in time brings her out in a sweat, and she racks her brain in order to undo what's already done.

And now Giovanna is in class, as she should be, biting her nails. Everything about her seems lovable. She didn't realize it immediately, but right beside the recent Giovanna is the one from the first year. That Giovanna puts two fingers in her mouth and brings out a milk tooth, places it in her palm, and looks at it wonderingly before putting it in her pocket.

Silvia can't bear to be alive in this world knowing that Giovanna is no more.

11

MARTINO WAS NEW AT SCHOOL. The year had begun a few weeks ago and he didn't have any friends. He tapped on his desk, pretending to play the piano even though he really didn't know how. But no one actually knew that and it was his way of pretending to be someone and demonstrating his own lack of interest in his classmates, who ignored him noisily, called each other nicknames from one side of the class to the other, passed round marbles and toy figurines, played sea battles or spluttered secrets into each other's ears, foreheads against temples.

Martino stayed focused, staring at his hands and using—or pretending to use—his little finger, the way he imagined professional pianists did. But he was actually listening to the buzz of voices and every now and then he glanced sideways at the row of desks close to the big windows to see if Giulia had noticed his display—and no, it seemed not at all: her profile, that of a sulky Madonna, was half hidden by her hair, and all he could see was her nose sticking out.

Martino didn't like his class and he didn't like Biella: the unfamiliar mountains, too close, and streets that were just streets, with no memories to bring them alive. Even the tap water had a funny taste, and every time he had a drink his mood soured. For him home was Turin, and his neighborhood, Borgo Vanchiglia, had hatched him like a mother hen. There wasn't a single crossing or building without some meaning for him in his neighborhood. He knew everyone by sight, even the dogs, and could predict around which corner they might lift a leg.

Martino and his mother had moved during summer because of his asthma. Lately, a hiss that sometimes accompanied his exhalation, and which as a child he'd called The Whistle, had become constant. The attacks began with a cough, a metallic one that scratched his throat and stopped him from expelling and then taking in enough air. He knew that at that point his bronchial tubes would contract and become inflamed. He pictured them thick and tough, like the hide of a hippopotamus. He couldn't even speak. At its worst, he had to put on an oxygen mask.

When there was no rain for weeks, the dust from factories, furnaces, and ducts saturated the air. Those were the years that saw the beginning of environmental protest, but in Turin very little was yet known, and it was only the workers' movement that started to concern itself with the concentration of toxic substances in factories. On top of that, people smoked everywhere, hopping on buses and trams without putting out their cigarettes. Teachers smoked in class, and at the cinema a fug of smoke veiled the screen. You could even smoke undisturbed in hospitals.

Martino, who'd always been asthmatic, read the magazines and books his mother brought home: he knew he was breathing in carbon monoxide, hydrochloric acid composed of fluoride, sulphur dioxide, tar, and nicotine.

"The least he could do is go to the country," his doctor ordered, "somewhere with a lot of greenery where the air is good." Which is how they ended up moving to live with a relative in the village of Bioglio. *Let's try it for a year*, they told him, *to see if your asthma gets better*. His father would join them on Friday evening and go back on Sunday. Rather than enrolling him in the tiny village school, which they were biased against since they were from Turin, they decided he would go to school in town.

Martino experienced it all as a sort of oppression. He'd have much preferred to die coughing in Turin, among the blackened doorways and trees freckled with dust that stuck to their leaves and trunks. Surrounded by his friends, Agostino and Piero and Roberto, all of whom had healthy lungs and couldn't care less about pollution.

12

When their teacher, Fogli, entered, the children quickly became quiet and Martino looked up from his imaginary piano. There was something unusual about the teacher's appearance, something saggy about her face and hairstyle; her movements were hesitant. She was young and athletic, and to play down both characteristics she'd adopted an unnaturally slow walk, wore a teased hairdo, and had a habit of sucking peppermints—moving them to one side of her mouth to explain something and then pausing in the middle of a lesson to crunch them between her teeth seemed to her the privilege of any teacher worth her salt.

That day she should have been teaching a lesson in math but instead she raised the issue of Misfortune—she called it that mentally, with a capital letter that stood for the capital G in Giovanna. She thumped her palm on the desk, though everyone was silent, touched her golden wedding ring, and saw her face reflected in it. She didn't know where to start. When the older members of her family died, one after another, she was the one who'd changed their beds and disinfected the final sheets with baking soda, the one who'd rolled up their carpets, sprinkled mothballs in their drawers, packed their things, and filled huge sacks with rubbish. She'd done all of those things quietly, vigorously; in fact, precisely because doing them meant she could stay quiet.

It must be easier for Sister Annangela, she thought. *It must be an entirely different matter. It's a good thing that she's going to Giovanna's class.*

She unwrapped a peppermint but immediately covered her mouth and spit it back into its paper, wrapped it well, and put it in the desk drawer, wiping her fingers on her skirt. Thank heavens the desk was paneled at the front and sides, a cheap wooden chest that protected her like a fortress. She decided she'd say only what was essential, and quickly. She apologized for being late and explained that there'd been unforeseen difficulties, a very sad event. Tragic.

"Unfortunately, a girl from the other year-six class has died. We found out this morning," she said.

She didn't add anything else apart from the girl's name, because a hand shot up: naturally, they asked. Saying Giovanna's name in front of the class was the most difficult thing she'd done since she'd gotten to school that morning; in fact, since she had become a teacher, and perhaps ever.

The thought somehow boosted her: of course she was in a difficult situation. How could it be otherwise? Even Sister Annangela was having difficulties: she was devastated, she was. It was just that she seemed to react a bit better than the others, but as she was a nun she must have certainties along with the strong character everyone recognized in her. After all, Annangela didn't have a family to burden her or whom she had to fear for more than anything else in the world. What could ever happen to her? She couldn't lose a husband, a child. Silvia couldn't either, and yet it had happened. Something had destroyed her. *She's not coming back tomorrow, they won't find her*, Fogli said to herself, and she felt it was true and was amazed by her sudden conviction: it was as if she'd caught a gnat in midair but distractedly, by chance and without even trying.

Praying seemed a respectable way of making the time go by. They recited the Hail Mary and the Eternal Rest, the prayer for the dead. The children moved their lips in unison and looked around, sizing each other up and matching their reactions. For many of them, the clearest thing was the excitement of a morning different from the usual. They were called upon to show their sorrow and they gave themselves over to it, imitating the mournful expressions of adults they'd seen at funerals.

Meanwhile, Fogli was giving some thought to what she should do with Giulia, because Giulia was the daughter of Anselmo, Silvia's cousin, and Fogli knew very well how close they were. Already she seemed the most disturbed of all the children, her gaze fixed and the corners of her mouth turned down.

Giulia looked like her mother, Luisa. Gemma, her grandmother, was a hard nut, but those two, no.

"You and your mother have a push button for tears," Anselmo would say. "The pair of you are crybabies." And now Giulia couldn't stop imagining the girl's death. She didn't know Giovanna and could barely recall her appearance—she was blond, she thought, and looked taller: whether coming or going, she stood out in the crowded entrance.

The teacher hadn't gone into detail, so Giulia kept her eyes glued to the blue-green paint on her desk where she saw the tragedy unfold, the one her father emphatically warned her against almost every day: crossing the road on a red light or without looking both ways several times and thus getting hit; taking a bad fall from her bicycle; leaning too far over the balcony; climbing a tree and the branch breaking under her weight; getting sick from eating poisonous berries or mushrooms; swimming in the river (whirlpools, or getting a cramp from indigestion); slipping and hitting her head while getting out of the bathtub; dropping the hairdryer in water; getting a shock from touching an electrical outlet or exposed wires.

It could easily have been me in Giovanna's place, she thought. Yet deep down, Giulia couldn't quite believe that. She was still a little girl, she thought she was special and the world owed her something: luck, some way out. All around, her classmates, too, were secretly relishing the morning light, hair they could touch and arrange with their hands, chairs squeaking over the floor, paper in their exercise books and agendas plastered with fingerprints that bore the pungent odor of ink and snacks. And they exchanged furtive glances shot through with the guilty relief of the survivor.

13

GIOVANNA'S EMPTY DESK attracted glances and then repelled them. It was like an open trapdoor in the classroom. Sister Annangela placed her bun-shaped hand on the shoulder of the little girl who had sat next to Giovanna and now sat by herself; she gave a little snort and then began sobbing, her eyes meanwhile staring in surprise because she hadn't expected to cry so soon, so suddenly and noisily. They all competed to console her, and the more comfort she got the more she cried, trails of shiny mucus running down the sleeves of her smock. When she calmed down, they went on to write letters to Giovanna's family, embellished with hearts and flowers. The ones who were best at drawing labored over angels with suffering faces: "We'll never forget you," "Rest in peace," "You're in heaven now," "Mother Mary, pray for Giovanna."

The collars of the little girls' smocks were wet with tears and they held fast to their handkerchiefs with their free hands. The children seemed bewildered and grim with embarrassment. They were on the alert, as if someone had suddenly handed them the leash of a big, unfamiliar dog.

They had permission to go to the loo in pairs to freshen up

and there was a procession. Two girls, encouraging each other, started to wail so loudly that they had to sit on the floor tiles to calm down, never mind the brown shoeprints or scraps of wet toilet paper. In the heat of the moment, they apologized for old grievances and hugged each other.

"You must forgive me."

"No, *you* must forgive *me*. You're my best friend."

A handful of journalists stood waiting at the school gates hoping to speak to the headmaster, maybe get some quotes to add to their pieces.

"You're a pain in the neck!" One father lost it.

Sister Annangela remained seated in her Fiat Cinquecento until the driveway and road were free. The sight of children coming out of the gates alive, schoolbags thumping, pierced the hearts of the parents; it couldn't be taken for granted, and it wouldn't be for some time to come. Sister Annangela needed to feel that mixture of panic, bewilderment, and love surging around her, every last drop of it. It would be helpful when she went to see Giovanna's mother and father.

14

MARTINO HEADED for the bus stop, dazed and hungry. The seats in the bus shelter were occupied by two older girls—from the lyceum, maybe—who were comparing the veins in their arms. One had green veins, the other lilac. They discussed them for some time and then moved on to their hair: who had more split ends? It seemed they even found strands split into three. Martino wasn't sure whether that was good or bad. He recognized the disgusting pleasure he felt when he saw a hairy spider scampering up the wall. He moved a few feet away and in imitation started looking at the scratches on the backs of his hands (a blackberry bush), the white marks on his nails.

During break they realized that Giovanna's teacher was also missing—all it took was for the year-six classes to meet in the playground. Sister Annangela crossed the cement drive, steering clear of the little ones from the second and third years playing football and tripping over their own feet. Tiny, round, and determined, she drew Giulia aside. Martino realized then that the teacher Canepa must be Giulia's relative, perhaps an aunt.

He could hardly bring her to mind. The question wasn't who she was, but what she was: a teacher, whose role it was to stay in class, explain things, give marks, and put notes in her diary. He struggled to recall something specific. Sister Annangela was friendly, but Canepa wasn't. She seemed distracted—not busy, just distracted. She wasn't pretty and she wasn't ugly, neither tall nor short. Her hair was brown and she wore simple clothes that always looked the same, like a uniform. She didn't make much of an impression.

On the bus, Martino sat a long way from the others. He wasn't going to give in: this wasn't his home and it was never going to become his home. He chewed belligerently on his salami sandwich and watched the famous green slide by, the green for which he'd come to live here, spotted with yellow, brown, and red. The trees and briars actually grew too much, overrunning paths, straying into the road, and weighing down rooftops, their roots splitting pavements and making the asphalt on the roads lumpy. The bus struggled along the windy route: it was turning around at the Rovella, at whose summit there were converging ridges covered with even thicker woods. Martino had no idea that his teacher had been born and lived for a long time in the village where he'd settled.

He got off at the stop in front of the church and passed the bar and the fountain. The house his mother, Lea, lived in had a typical Piedmontese façade with wooden shutters at the windows, paneled balconies and corbels in stone from Lucerne, wrought-iron railings. At the back was a garden with tall grass, a pergola with wisteria climbing over it, and a big persimmon tree loaded with fruit, round as bowling balls. When they set foot in it for the first time, Lea had scrutinized the crazy plants, hands at her sides.

"What a jungle!" she said. And of the wisteria: "Well, that will become a violet cloud in the spring." Then she gestured toward the persimmons with her chin. "And on that one we'll see a lot of little suns in a month's time. Do you hear me, Grumpy?"

He found her right there, hanging up the washing. She snapped it like a whip and hung it on the line with a peg shaped like a soldier. She fished a tablecloth from the basket, and when she saw him she smiled.

"Come and help me."

Martino threw his schoolbag to the ground and started shaking out the wet pillowcases. It was a good way of venting the anger he felt at finding himself in that place and the turmoil caused by the girl's death which he now felt brewing in his stomach. For him it was the umpteenth proof that the decision to leave Turin had been disastrous, a catastrophe it was impossible to get used to. He hoped that all the persimmons would fall down together in a shower, splattering over the laundry like water balloons. The hair on the backs of his arms stood up. His mother noticed it.

"Wait, what is it?"

"Nothing."

"Oh, come on. Tell me."

They went on like this for a while until Martino shouted, "I don't want to be here! Kids die here!"

Lea was flabbergasted. "What do you mean?"

"A girl from the other class died," he managed to add before running inside. As she followed him up the stairs, Lea asked herself if someone at work knew but hadn't said anything about it. She'd managed to get a job as a secretary at the Biella knitwear factory in Pettinengo, where she transferred phone calls and kept papers, correspondence, and index files in order. The place had its own grim fascination. It was a huge bastion of industry constructed more than a century before, and from there it towered over the entire plain of Biella. She realized instantly that her new colleagues found her brusque and disagreeable, given her way of dealing with any duty quickly and well—like a robot—to get it out of the way as soon as she could. Yet though Lea had worked for more than ten years as a receptionist at a hair salon on Corso Francia in Turin, she didn't miss it at all. The fact that she had red hair—a flaming red that looked as though it came from a bottle—didn't help, and neither did the fact that she'd moved only with her son, and hadn't brought her husband along.

Martino was sitting at the desk with a comic book in front of him, *The Ballad of the Salty Sea*. He wished he had sideburns like the sailor, Corto Maltese. The earring, no; that was a step too far. He wouldn't have been seen as half-sailor, half-pirate, but a poofter to be roughed up. The corners of his eyes stung with tears that wanted release. His mother came to hug him from behind with the chairback between them, but she towered over him all the same. She rested her chin and neck on his head and breathed into his hair and he felt once more secure, as if he were inside a treasure chest.

15

GIOVANNA PLACES a large branch from a pine tree in Silvia's arms. The needles prick the teacher's hands; it seems like a stiff brush rather than a pine, the sort you use for scraping dried mud off your shoes.

"For science, Miss." This is a strange Giovanna with wet hair, much longer than she's ever had. "I took a shower," she explains, though the teacher hadn't dared to ask.

Silvia looks at her, loving her, fearing her.

"Pines have long needles, but they're in clusters . . . or in pairs. Right?"

Silvia nods, never taking her eyes off Giovanna.

"Spruce have short needles, all along the branch."

Drops of water fall on Giovanna's face from her fringe, which is soaking wet.

"The cones on a spruce are long and soft. The ones on pines are round and woody," she continues, shifting her weight from one foot to the other.

Silvia makes out a figure standing in the doorway. It's a woman she recognizes only because she kept the photographs. It's her mother. Giovanna turns, following her gaze, and says to the woman, “Shoo! shoo!” and she moves to block Silvia’s view of the door. She’s holding her textbook but that, too, is drenched, its pages wavy and soft, paper jelly.

“That’s it, I’m not keeping this anymore,” Giovanna says. “I might as well throw it away.”

She lets it fall. Now it’s a multicolored aspic jelly, a display case of fat filled with chicken, hard-boiled egg, and vegetables that breaks into three or four sticky pieces and rolls in earth and twigs.

Silvia is hungry.

16

GIULIA FOUND HER PARENTS at home when she got back from school. Anselmo became hysterical, and during the brief moments when he was quiet it was even worse: he paced the room, taking long steps, and transmitted anxiety like a human television antenna. To Giulia it seemed as if the waves were spreading and vibrating in her chest, a toxic weight of pain accumulated and stored behind her ribs. But it wasn't long before her father exploded in a new tirade against Minero from the newsstand; the headmaster and Sister Annangela, who hadn't phoned him immediately; and the forces of order and others who had absolutely nothing to do with it.

A pair of journalists came to the entryphone and he welcomed them in his way: shouting and swearing. He didn't want to get the Carabinieri too involved because he considered them roughneck southerners, slowcoaches. He advised them to be careful and told them that he himself would help out with the search since he knew the area and the missing person very well. The priest was invited in only because Gemma and Luisa were ready to do battle on that point and they had become like martyrs on the gridiron. He was old, eighty and counting, with warts on his eyelids and rimming his eyes. If he'd been a young priest, they might not have sprouted. Don Luigi urged them to have faith and pray, especially to St. John the Baptist of La Salle, the patron saint of teachers, while Anselmo snorted like a bull and busied himself pouring a glass of absinthe.

Luisa got on the phone and called the city hospital and places Silvia might have gone by bus or train, but no one had admitted a woman answering to her description: injured, unconscious, mute. Struck with amnesia, driven mad with sorrow. It was good news—but also bad. She closed the phone book, fighting the urge to cry that was rising in her throat: she gave it her all. She didn't want to frighten Giulia further.

Gemma turned the meatballs over in butter. They'd come out badly, lumpy and misshapen. The table was laid but no one wanted to sit down apart from five-year-old Corrado. He asked who Silvia was and was satisfied with an evasive reply. He was now hopping around Grandma, trying to convince her to give him a piece of meat straight from the wooden spoon.

Giulia hid her concern much better than Luisa. She helped Corrado cut up his meatballs with the fork and at one point she gave her mother a forced smile. Silvia, she thought, would have wiped the browned butter off the bottom of the saucepan with a piece of bread—she loved butter, oil, melted cheese, greasy crusts left in pans.

Giulia loved her a lot, and in particular the character traits the family scolded her for. Silvia knew better than anyone how to shut out the noise of Anselmo's bickering, to the extent that when she was minding her own business she didn't answer even if you asked her something. She'd had an appointment one afternoon to go to the land registry with Anselmo. He didn't want to go upstairs so he called from the street until he was hoarse: "Silvia, Silvia! Are you deaf? Silvia! The land registry!" Louder and louder, more and more exasperated. Giulia had wanted to put her fingers in her ears, but Silvia just sat there cutting out an article on Princess Grace of Monaco from *Christian Family* magazine, and she'd kept on going until she realized that someone was yelling downstairs. Without looking up she said, "Your father is calling you, can't you hear?"

"Look, *you're* Silvia!" Giulia got her attention.

"Ah, so I am." She put down the scissors, slipped on her coat and loafers, and went downstairs, unruffled.

She could ignore entire conversations without even using wax earplugs. But she'd focus completely when she felt like it and it was one-on-one. It made no difference if her interlocutor was a child: she gave you her undivided attention and made you feel like Scheherazade (Giulia owned a sumptuously illustrated edition of *The Thousand and One Nights*, and it was her favorite book). Silvia remembered that type of conversation, and would later ask for news and updates. She never gave advice. The only thing she stubbornly repeated to young people who ventured into her realm was "Study!", pronouncing it with the closed Piedmontese "u."

Giulia also sensed that Silvia had a problem: she felt too much a guest. She ate supper with them every evening, but it was just that—with them, in their family: she was on the edge. Nevertheless, Silvia and Anselmo were much more like siblings than cousins. Their grandparents had brought them up together since Silvia was an orphan and Anselmo's parents had neglected him, a child between the firstborn, who was in delicate health, and the third: pretty and bossy.

Silvia's disappearance had plunged Anselmo into fear, or rather a rage. It was fear of the sort he couldn't find any way to off-load, not even by having it out with everyone, slamming doors or punching walls. He'd organized a search in the woods for the next day starting from Bioglio, the village he and Silvia were from. He opened a map on the table beside his plate of meatballs to study the best route. There would be about ten of them, and five or six obedient hunting dogs. Now and then he'd dunk a stick of celery in the *pinzimonio*, then insult the drops of oil he dropped on the map.

Giulia wasn't as good as Silvia at exempting herself and she'd had enough that night. She asked for permission to go to bed and huddled under the covers with *The Thousand and One Nights*.

Luisa came to turn out the lights around nine.

"It'll all be okay," she whispered. She didn't actually believe it.

Giulia wished she could tell her to stuff it, but she said, "Sure, Mamma." It was the artificial utterance of an adult, and Luisa realized that it matched her own. Her daughter hid her feelings, preferring to keep them quiet and let things go, which meant she was growing up. She wished she could share that internal excitement, but she knew that slowly—with any luck very slowly—she'd be excluded and would have to be okay with it.

She stroked Giulia's arm. "Sweetheart, we can't do anything besides look for her and hope."

Luisa realized with dismay that they hadn't talked about Giovanna. Overwhelmed as they were by Silvia's disappearance, they'd neglected the girl. She looked at her own daughter, a child, little bumps under the covers and the sober expression of a hieroglyph. She had to admit that no parent could fathom what Giovanna had done, not at her age. She was too young to foresee the consequences, to understand that she would cease to exist after leaping into the river. That she wouldn't be able to get out on the bank, walk home, ring the bell, and stand dripping on the doormat. Maybe she'd jumped because of that failure to understand. Because she hadn't realized that she would die.

17

Boarding school. It comes back to her with extraordinary clarity and it's much more real than the rain dripping on her from the leaky roof. All the same, Silvia puts out her tongue to quench her thirst: it's thick and dry like cardboard. It takes her back once more to boarding school, to the brown blankets they used.

They slept in big dormitories and made their beds every morning according to instructions, which were to tuck the sheets and blankets in so tight that getting in would be difficult. There was nothing soft about those cots. Inside the rectangle of the mattress were the pillow's rectangle, the rectangle of the tucked-in sheets, the rectangle of the brown blanket. They got in, huffing and puffing with effort. The bed was supposed to be a sheath where the bodies of little girls and older girls were put back every night. They were to have no space to scratch themselves, bend their knees, or touch themselves freely. Nightgowns were wide and stiff, beds narrow and hard, and the combination a carefully considered effort to hinder and prevent.

Silvia sees her classmates, other boarders. Some remained good friends, but now they crowd around her just as they were in those years: girls in uniform, their knees pale orbs between tall socks and skirts, young, immature faces behind curtains of hair. Among those girls from another time is Giovanna, a girl forever, and together they watch as if Silvia were an exotic specimen trapped in a cage.

Sitting on the ground, she scoots backward just far enough to get out of the rain, into a corner of the hut that's undamaged. Giovanna still has damp hair clinging to her skull, which is why logic is flashing on and off in Silvia's mind and with it a feeble sense of time. The fact is that before (how long before? impossible to say), before, Silvia didn't believe the story of the shower. She knows when a child is lying and she's certain (she was certain) that it was the river water in which Giovanna drowned that made her soaking wet. Now, though, she wonders whether it isn't the same rainwater falling on both of them. And if they are in the same rain, then Silvia is dead, too, and her visions are the ones that come *after*. She needs to go over everything, piece by piece, the whole muddle. Everything: Giovanna's death as well, and Silvia tenses up because she hears the phone shrieking again, and she waits to hear the receiver being picked up.

But then she notices that the boarders are dry. Only Giovanna is wet, but it doesn't seem to her (she looks hard) that there are any new drops falling on her. For the first time, Silvia wonders whether the opposite is true: maybe she's alive after all, and the girls aren't really there. "There" is where it's raining, and what she's absorbing at that moment is true, it's real. She struggles to make a list: herself, the straw, the branches waving inside and outside the hut, the walls darkened with the damp. Those things, though, don't interest her, which is why they retreat and become dim.

On the other hand, her school returns very clearly. The beds, her classmates, the refectory, the smell of soup and insecticide, the parlor where they met their families and where the orphans were spectators of the Great Mystery: having a mother. How a mother kisses you, how she ignores you. Some mothers were inattentive even on that one day of the week.

Silvia once heard one of them whispering to her little girl, "Don't you dare whine. There'll be trouble if you do," and she was as offended as if that unjust telling-off had been directed at her.

On Sundays, the parlor. Her grandmother with flesh-colored tights rucked up around her ankles, like the skin on certain dogs. Her elegant grandfather, with his hat and well-cut jacket, his gilet and the handkerchief in his pocket. Her grandmother was losing her hair. And she wasn't the person who'd given birth to her. This was important, she always said to her friend Marilena, who was left with only her aunts on her father's side. Marilena is actually there beside Silvia, and she touches her tummy below her navel like pregnant women do.

"Well, come on," she says. "Your grandmother is your mother's mother after all."

But Silvia is disgusted by the idea that her mother came out of her grandmother's stomach in the big sleigh bed, its headboard inlaid with leaves and scrolls and Grandfather's initials in the center: CC, Costantino Canepa. She herself often slept in it beside Grandmother, tucking the covers in tight so they wouldn't fall down. At home as at school, she could expect a cocooned sleep.

Now Marilena's round gray eyes are shining, and this means she's arrived: Antonia's mother, queen of Sunday visits. Silvia doesn't remember the name of that beautiful woman anymore, blond with high cheekbones, wide nose, and invisible eyebrows, the cougar-mother, but again she sees the two cups she used to carry with her, carefully wrapped in newspaper (octagonal goblets, their rims outlined in gold), and the tin of powdered chocolate to be added to milk. She and her daughter Antonia say, "Chin-chin!" and drink. The mother whimpers, "I miss you. I miss you so much," and Silvia understands why Antonia is upset by those bursts of affection, which only end up making her emotionally impoverished school life more difficult.

"I don't believe that. You can't miss me so much if you leave me here," Antonia begins, and her mother takes pains to deny it and explain everything before a cowardly phrase slips out.

"Your father is inflexible."

But Antonia isn't appeased. She wants her mother to go away in torment as she herself is tormented by having to stay, but then she regrets it the moment her mother turns the corner. She runs her tongue around her mouth trying to taste the last bit of chocolate and looks at Silvia and Marilena because they've witnessed the scene and they're orphans. They're worse off than she is.

18

IT HAD BEEN RAINING for hours and was still dark. Sitting in her car, Luisa watched the red and white lights go past distorted by the rain, and the fixed yellow of the streetlamps. In the factory car park she took advantage of the rain to close the car door quickly and take shelter. Anselmo was more ill-tempered than ever because they were going to have to search in the rain, with nervous dogs and reduced visibility. They both thought about the sodden ground, swelling rivers, and wet clothes that chill a body quickly. But Silvia could be inside somewhere—or at least able to drink something.

The factory where Luisa worked made intimates: vests, underwear, pajamas, socks, and pantyhose. The workers and office employees were all women and they had lockers where they could leave their coats and handbags. When she went into the cloakroom the heads of women fiddling with locks, scarves, or a thermos of tea went up in unison and she prepared to be surrounded.

"Any news?"

"Good heavens, it's raining today too."

"Let's hope she's inside somewhere."

"She couldn't take it, poor thing."

"Well it's hardly her fault."

"Silvia is an extraordinary teacher."

Luisa nodded politely. She understood that they were genuinely worried and that the constant repetition allowed them to breathe freely. And you couldn't deny it—it kept them excited, banished boredom. Silvia was the theme of the day. An odd but unassuming woman who had shunned attention all her life but ended up attracting it by disappearing. People were going over various events in her life, her appearance, her commitment, her solitary nature. Luisa understood the paradox and felt it her duty to protect Silvia from gossip, but she was too polite to be effective. Then something made her blood boil.

"Well, it's understandable. A single person without loved ones?" a woman with backcombed hair was saying: Mariachiara. "She got more attached to her students than she should have. I'm not sure how to explain it. Kind of obsessively. I mean, they're all she has. And it's a great thing, right? That sort of teacher. Everyone knows it. But then something bad happens and you go crazy. My mother-in-law knows her well and says she wasn't quite right even as a girl."

"Mariachiara!" Luisa cried, and suddenly she was stunned. She should have let it go, but she felt her face burning right up to the tips of her ears and she walked up to the gaggle of women. She never lost her cool; she was in uncharted territory. Over the years, she'd outsourced all her anger to Anselmo. *Stupid idiot*, she thought, referring to herself as well as Mariachiara. She didn't know how to get out of this.

"Oh, Luisa. I know. It must be awful for all of you," Mariachiara hurriedly added, sounding distressed.

Luisa was ready to step backward, offer a conciliatory smile, and start her shift.

"We all love Silvia. I'm only saying—"

"What?"

"Oh, nothing, only that if Fernanda or Bruna had disappeared into thin air, or you, for that matter, I really would be surprised. But Silvia has always been a little unusual, no? In a good way."

Luisa could smell Mariachiara's toxic hair spray; her look seemed poisonous too. She spotted white and silver hairs on her black raincoat.

"If you say so," she cut her off. Fortunately not many were listening. But by that point she couldn't stop herself.

"Listen, Mariachiara, actually you need to do something about that cat smell. It's really nasty. I think he's sprayed your raincoat; you know how they mark things."

She left Mariachiara sniffing her clothes with a resentful expression that made her ugly.

Sometimes, at moments like those, Luisa asked herself what she was doing there, and by *there* she meant her life. It wasn't a nice thing to say, and in fact she didn't say it—she didn't dare follow the thought through. She felt as though her children were fully hers. Giulia was sweet as pie and it didn't seem like she was the type to go badly off the rails during adolescence, so long as Anselmo didn't become so unbearable that he pushed her to leave with the first moron who came along. Corrado, the little one, was a real pest. Her mother, Gemma, had treated him like a prince since he was a boy, not bothering to teach him things Giulia could do very well at his age.

Luisa could guess where her sense of irrelevance came from, just as she could work out the deep reasons that had led her to marry Anselmo. It was because of what had happened twenty-six years before, during the war. She had heard about people surviving with shrapnel throughout their bodies, actual bullets in their skulls that couldn't be removed. She saw herself like that: with something inside, or rather something cold and hard at her center that she'd managed to heal over despite herself. Something, however, that had broken her down and left part of her numb.

Luisa was nostalgic for the Friuli of her youth, though she would have found it difficult, if not impossible, to live there. The countryside lay open to the sky without being contained by mountains, an expanse of greens and yellows: tobacco, sweet corn, wheat. For her, mountains had always had a pressing aspect, like a belt that squeezes too hard at your waist. She preferred to have as much sky over her as possible, as far as the eye could see. Friulian polenta was white, a full moon sliced with a length of cotton thread; once cold, it served as breakfast and snack. At dawn, the mist rising from the River Tagliamento rippled images, so that the entire landscape looked like a dream. Luisa had many pleasant memories. But she fell in love during the war in the very worst months of 1944. That was when she'd started to nibble at the skin around her nails, leaving the flesh red, bare, and painful. All of her felt like that, without the necessary protective layer, without the bark. That was why she tore away at her cuticles: to make them more like the rest of her.

Luisa's family was with the partisans and that made her proud. The boy she was in love with, though, had a brother with the republicans. He wasn't fascist himself but he loved his brother, a Blackshirt, all the same. The partisans locked him in a barn for questioning: they wanted him to betray his brother or help them to find him—they might execute him or use him as a prisoner exchange. Luisa never knew if they shot him in frustration, in error, or merely on impulse because he tried to escape.

It was the partisans who did it and the entire universe stopped for her. She knew them well: names, faces, and families. The family were often with her—older cousins or friends of cousins, classmates, fishing mates, friends from the army. She'd left sacks of potatoes, new shoelaces, and woolen berets in ditches for them, put on three or four jumpers, one on top of another, and tied them tightly to branches at the edge of the thickets. She'd begged them to get the Nazis out and she continued to do so. If it had been the Germans, at least she could have exhausted herself hating them.

Gemma hadn't noticed. She'd said, "That's just how it is right now. We're all suffering like dogs." Luisa didn't have the strength to explain how she felt, and probably not even the words to do so. People hadn't gotten used to talking about their own pain and no one set much stock by the feelings of adolescents—too flighty and illogical. She had panic attacks called air-hunger. "Luisa is hungry for air," they'd say, "clear some space. Let her sit down."

It happened whenever she remembered the last time she'd seen the boy she'd fallen in love with (could she call him "my boyfriend"? He'd declared his feelings, but it wasn't official and they'd only just kissed). Luisa was walking along the mill path. He was in the kitchen garden at his house, standing on a chair between rows and picking beans, tossing them into a bucket at his feet: *plunk, plunk, plunk* from his position up high. She hadn't called out to him; she'd wanted to watch him through the trellis and leaves where she was hiding. Swallows scissored low through the air. The beans were mottled, purple and white.

Later, before she went home, Luisa took a moment by herself to read the newspaper. It had stopped raining, the low, compact layer of clouds had broken apart, and the light was continually changing color from gray to pink, pink to gray. There were various articles about Giovanna and Silvia.

First the tragedy of the child, now the mystery of the teacher.

Eleven-year-old drowns herself, teacher disappears.

Numerous theories, no light on shocking event.

Fears of another reckless act.

On the second page they'd published a photograph of Silvia chosen by Luisa, hoping that someone, somewhere, would recognize her. It had also appeared in *La Stampa* in Turin. The photo had been taken in the spring and they'd been in a meadow in Bioglio; looking at it, you caught the scent of new grass and sun-baked dust. Silvia was looking straight into the lens, yet even so she gave the impression of being a spectator rather than the subject of the photo. Luisa had had to cut herself out at the side but a slice of her shoulder remained, the crook of her elbow.

Underneath, a long article explained how Giovanna had often skipped school and on the day of the tragedy her teacher, Canepa, had decided to let the family know. "This could be one reason for the suicide and the subsequent disappearance of the teacher. However, both facts plunge too deeply into the dark recesses of the human psyche for the theory to have any validity when considered logically, even in a superficial and makeshift way."

On the contrary: Luisa believed she understood Silvia. When it had been her turn to suffer she hadn't run off to hide—but only because she hadn't felt guilty. Unlike Silvia. If Silvia wasn't dead and she wasn't coming back, then she didn't want to be found.

19

PEOPLE SHOUTING, dogs yapping in the distance. It sounds like there are a lot of them, calling *Silvia!* perhaps. But that's no concern of hers. She's no longer certain about answering to that name, barely recognizes it, as if it were a foreign word whose meaning she grasps only obliquely. She has a premonition, though, that the shouting and yapping are forerunners in a series of events: being seen by human eyes, picked up, put in a car and then a bathtub. She doesn't comprehend these circumstances in a separate and linear way but as a generic fumbling of hands and voices in a sack. And she is that sack.

With immense effort she drags herself out in the driving rain, and everything goes dark and indistinct.

She opens her eyes again. Her nostrils are full of mud; she spits some out of her mouth. She starts crawling again and plants herself under a blackberry bush which has grown into the hazelnut copse. She lies there in the thick of it where no one can save her.

When the silence swells to reclaim the woods, she crawls back inside the hut.

20

GIANNI WAS THE ONLY FRIEND Lea and Martino had in Bioglio. He was a distant cousin—third or fourth—and before they moved they'd only bumped into him at a couple of weddings; he and Lea had barely exchanged ten words. They regretted never having gotten together previously, because friendship blossomed instantly.

Gianni worked at the knitwear factory, too, though in export since he spoke English so well. He was tall and skinny with a nose like an upturned mushroom, thin lips, cheeks marred with pits and laugh lines, a crew cut. He was always saying he was ugly but Martino wasn't convinced. Gianni wasn't at all ugly. He would have been the unlucky gunslinger or a gravedigger in a Western, the guy who saves the hero by hiding him in a coffin at just the right moment.

When Gianni came by for a coffee he'd pat his shirt pocket every so often looking for a cigarette. Lea would glare at him, glance at Martino, and gesture toward the door with her chin. He'd shake his head and sign with his index finger: *I'll smoke later.*

Mostly they talked about books. Gianni wrote short stories that Lea feverishly read in a night, finding them beautiful. For the first time in her life she was friends with a writer; she might have felt intimidated, but since Gianni seemed intimidated by her, the two embarrassments ended up canceling each other out.

Sometimes Gianni would recite Milton or Gerard Manley Hopkins from memory, and he'd then translate on the spot.

"If you want to translate a poem, Martino, you have to pay attention to how it scans, to the enjambment, that is. En-jam-be-ment," he'd say. To please him, Martino scanned "en-jam-be-ment," even though it wasn't really his dream to start translating poetry. At school he'd been forced to memorize Carducci, and he'd found it super boring.

Gianni, though, made him see words in a new light, and it was as if Martino realized how to use them for the first time in his life. When he'd broken his wrist two summers ago, he'd needed physio to relearn how to use it: in practice, he'd sit and look at it for many minutes, until it softened like a squid as he rotated and bent it, all the while thinking, *Hey! Look what a wrist can do—a bunch of stuff*. He felt something similar with Gianni and his poetry, though words were even more useful than a wrist: they helped him to talk, to ask things. He thought it all through.

When he got going, Gianni would say, "*Glory be to God for dappled things, For skies of couple-color as a brinded cow* . . . For skies spotted like a cow! Well, look at this sky—how does it seem to you? Hm! It's paved with clouds." And Martino imagined himself, head down like a bat, making for a patch of gray sky.

"You show off, Gianni! What a performance!" Lea teased.

"You haven't heard a thing yet," he replied, and he began reciting John Donne:

Dull sublunary lovers' love
(Whose soul is sense) cannot admit
Absence, because it doth remove
Those things which elemented it.

"So who are those sublunaries?" Martino asked. He imagined them as bald aliens on a flying saucer.

"They're us, young man. You are a sublunar boy."

"We, who love foolishly," Lea commented, and Gianni smiled at the wall.

That afternoon, Martino realized that Gianni was worrying about the missing teacher and wasn't looking at the sky in order to find similes but to determine whether it was really clearing up or was starting to rain again as it had the day before, all night, and that morning too. Their garden was watered by the rain. The water was still gushing through the guttering and several persimmons had finally come down.

"What's it like at school without Silvia? Miss Canepa, I mean."

"She's not my teacher. There's a stand-in. I don't know. Everyone's sad."

"What about the search?" Lea asked Gianni.

"Around here—nothing. We were hopeful, but: nothing. If she's in the area, she's not responding to anyone's calls. There's some hope that she might have gotten on a train and left."

"But do you know her well?" Lea asked.

"Very well. We were children together. She's younger than me, though, by at least four years."

All at once Martino thought of searching the woods. It seemed like a mission, an adventure. He could be the one to find the teacher and win the respect of Gianni, his mother, the entire school, and Giulia, that swot. After a feat like that, he'd be able to convince his family to go back to Turin. You don't deny a hero a return to his own country. He would penetrate the evil green of Bioglio as he would the scrub of an island populated by cannibals or the heart of the black jungle. A cross between the pirate Sandokan and the sailor Corto Maltese. "Ballad of the Dripping Forest," Gianni had written. He went to get his raincoat and a walking stick.

"I'm going out for a while."

"That's a novelty."

During the previous weeks Martino had done everything he could to block out the external world and avoid puncturing the bubble of Turinese images he was living in.

"Well don't go far. And don't forget your spray," Lea added. She meant his inhaler.

"I'll take a short stroll while it's not raining."

"Okay. Do you want to take a snack with you?"

Provisions weren't a bad idea. While he was making himself a butter and sugar sandwich, Martino overheard Gianni saying to his mother, "You know, I just hope she hasn't gone crazy with sorrow. I hope they don't find her half dead with hunger and off her head. That's all we need. Silvia in a mental institution."

"Weren't you saying that her family are nice people? They wouldn't do that to her."

"No, it's true. But they're not the ones doing the psychiatric evaluations."

A madwoman with hair erupting all over her head and a loose nightgown, that's what really scared Martino. Like the wife of that Englishman who rightly locked her up in an attic . . . Bertha . . . Bertha Mason. His mother had told him the story. And to top it off Bertha was a crazy pyromaniac. Did he feel like looking for someone who was already headed down that path? Corto Maltese wouldn't have given it a second thought. Sandokan, goes without saying. The main thing was, his teacher Canepa, as far as he remembered, wouldn't hurt a fly. It was this thought that pushed him out of the door, onto the shiny grass and beyond. Into the woods, which dripped cheerfully on his head.

21

THE WOODS WERE FILLED with the scent of resin and living wood. He felt it flood his lungs and oxygenate his hippopotamus hide, thinning it down. At first it seemed he was betraying Turin, but then he told himself that his expedition was the same as a Sunday walk in the mountains.

Worms had been forced to the surface where the rain had turned everything swampy. Martino knew why: it was to do with their breathing. Worms absorb oxygen through their skin, so if the rain floods the earth tunnels they live in, they must come out—or suffocate. He knelt to stir around with the end of his stick, stifling the desire to chop them into pieces provoked by the colors of their guts: pinkish, nude, and purple with microscopic rings, bulges, and swellings along the length of their stringy bodies.

From where he was crouched on the ground, he saw two hairy caterpillars latch on to a blade of grass. Beetles emerged from holes in the bark and ran over it like small metal cars, swerving around the protuberances and the gray fungus species that are one with their trees. Those he willingly battered with his stick; at any rate, they didn't break. He watched a woodpecker bore into a beech in search of larvae: it ate the larvae and the larvae ate the wood. A couple of times Martino ended up with his face in a spider's web. He tore up a fern and turned it over, noting the brown traces of spores.

He was distracted, not really looking for anything. He picked up a few pine cones and threw them like hand grenades, making the sound of an explosion with his mouth. He poked at globular grayish puffballs to see their powdery clouds, singing to himself, "Wolf farts! Wolf farts!" He poked at the white-blistered umbrellas of toadstools, too. Then he started using his stick as a sword against swarms of his comic-book Thugs. The tall grass wrapped itself around him and detained him, branches crisscrossing like real duelers. He battled against the locusts threatening him with their green spurs.

He became winded and had to slow down. He patted the pocket of his raincoat: his inhaler was there, in its place. It was in fact the magic potion given to him by a shaman as a sign of gratitude following a heroic exploit: for the record, the rescue of his only daughter, who'd been captured by enemies. At this point, he recalled his mission and climbed farther, right up to the semi-abandoned chapel. There was a small jar behind the iron grille but the flowers had dried up and been rained on. The Black Madonna in the niche was fading and had grown a ridiculous beard of moss. The baby, also black, looked like a miniature adult with goggle eyes. *Whoever painted them was awful*, thought Martino.

The vegetation became confused from that point onward. Brambles had colonized the undergrowth and no one came to cut wood or gather walnuts, hazelnuts, and chestnuts. Martino found it tiring to walk, but rather than holding him back it encouraged him because he imagined himself once more in the jungle. He came upon a small clearing and saw places where the grass and leaves had been trampled. He didn't know it, but those were prints left by roe deer who went there to sleep. A little farther on he recognized the shape of a hut, a sort of stable besieged by trees. A Thugs' bivouac. He crept up to it stealthily, brandishing his stick.

He intended to proceed by the rule book. The first thing to do was peep inside and get an idea of the enemy forces, even though he would jump right in anyway and slaughter everyone: the greater the number of assassins waiting to strangle him, the greater the glory. He took off his scarf and knotted it over his head like a turban. He was ready.

He peeped inside and immediately leapt backward, flung from his fantasy. He gasped in surprise, his chest gripped by a single spasm without release. He felt compelled to flee but would have to catch his breath first. He couldn't have an asthma attack there in the middle of the woods. He stepped away from the door and leaned against the boards of the hut, groping in his pocket for the spray. He inhaled the stream several times, blood thundering in his ears.

This wasn't like playing, when he trembled with fear in the belief that he could see the Thugs or Apaches even though they weren't real. There was someone in there. All the same, when he went back to lean in (as little as possible), he hoped he was wrong, that he had mistaken a sack or a pile of hay for a person.

He saw hair, a face, a jumper, a skirt. The missing teacher was only two steps away from him. Alive. He hid again and counted up to ten as his mother made him do when she wanted him to calm down (it never worked). Then he thought, *holysmoke, holysmoke, holysmoke, holysmoke*, clenching his teeth and bunching his fists. Things seemed a little better, but he still couldn't believe his eyes. He closed them, pressing his thumbs against them to make sure they were working, and then removed his thumbs. The light behind his eyelids flooded with red. Little by little, the woods came into focus along with his shoes, caked with earth and darkened with moisture. It wasn't a dream. She really was there.

He decided to peer in again, and he noticed that the teacher had remained in exactly the same static position, as if dazed. She was spellbound, her eyes cloudy, and it made him think of their neighbor's dog on the landing in Turin, blind from glaucoma. But that wasn't all. The teacher stank. Martino dared to laugh from tension, bewilderment, and disgust. Silvia Canepa smelled of piss, sweat, and musty clothes: it was a rancid smell, distinct from other ones in the woods. Martino wanted to plug his nose but he wasn't brave enough and anyway, with his condition it wouldn't do to block his airways.

He wondered whether he should say something, try to speak to her. *What do you say to a teacher who's hiding and stinks of piss?*

No, he decided, *I'll have to call for help*, and instantly he imagined running down at breakneck speed to raise the alarm. *I've found her!* and then fighting against his mother's and the other adults' skepticism, riding on Gianni's hopes, showing them the spot and from a distance, watching the first rescue workers enter the hut and come out a little later carrying the teacher, covered with a blanket. His back would be sore from all the pats and his cheeks would be worn out from smiling at all the compliments. *Yes, I went out just so I could find her. I went into the middle of the woods all by myself and discovered the hut.*

A rush of pride filled his belly. The next day at school: the hallways overflowing with admiration, small talk crackling like campfires at break time, and him in a corner twinkling modestly. Sister Annangela, Miss Fogli, the head all sending for him, thanking him. Giulia approaching him timidly and surely feeling the emotion, murmuring her thanks. *If it hadn't been for you . . .*

He looked in one last time to see if the teacher was injured. How long had it been since she'd eaten? Why wasn't she dead already? She'd drunk rainwater; that must have kept her going. But she didn't even have the strength to sit up anymore. Her head drooped over her chest in rhythm with her breathing.

He heard Gianni's voice once more: *I hope she hasn't gone crazy with grief* . . . and something about a mental institution and doctors. Martino imagined doctors and nurses holding enormous syringes like in a cartoon from *Puzzles Weekly*. Well, surely he should call for help. Better a mental institution than a cemetery.

With sudden inspiration, he took the butter sandwich out of his pocket. He didn't dare approach her, really didn't dare. It was quite something that he hadn't run away already. So he threw it toward her as gently as he could, trying not to give her a fright or awaken some violent act of madness—who knows?

Silvia squinted and rubbed her forehead dully, as if a chunk of meteorite had just fallen beside her. She raised her head very slowly and focused. A boy at the entrance to the hut. A terrified child who would uproot her from the woods and prevent her from starving. She hadn't spoken for who knows how long: her mouth wouldn't respond. Martino read the effort in her face and tensed up in return, ready to bolt. The teacher opened and closed her lips like an asthmatic, bubbles of saliva forming at the corners of her mouth.

"Don't tell anyone!" she breathed. Then she went back into her shell.

22

HE CAME DOWN THE HILLTOP like an avalanche, sweeping away the shrubs. With each stride it felt like his legs were about to detach from his body; his muscles were inflamed, blood pounded in his temples. He wanted to scream. He had to stop, bent double by a stitch, his fingertips pressing in below his ribs. Afterward he forced himself to walk in a more measured way. He was in danger of getting lost and taking too long to get home. The birds called out to one another from branch to branch, and beneath the foliage the light had faded and filled with dust particles. It wasn't long before sunset.

When the vegetation thinned out and he spotted the first houses of his village, Martino slowed down rather than speeding up, aware that he was hesitating, uncertain how to act. He was rattled. He'd found the missing teacher. He'd found her! It wasn't the moment to play the coward. He shook his head to banish those words of hers whirling around inside it like gnats: *Don't tell anyone!*

The teacher was dying. He couldn't leave her there. Why didn't she want help? She *needed* help. If you see someone about to shoot themselves you try to get them to change their mind, and if you can you throw yourself at them to stop them pulling the trigger. This was the same thing. But the teacher was dying little by little. She wasn't doing *anything*; in fact, she was staying absolutely still, turning into a plant, part of the woods. Martino had read somewhere that when Eskimos are old and death is nigh, they go off by themselves into the frozen wastelands and let the cold carry them away. Only she wasn't that old. Her situation must be different.

Well, she's crazy, he said to himself, *why am I standing here thinking about it? She's crazy. What she asked of me doesn't count. She's got a screw loose.*

For starters, to stink like that she must have peed herself. Only the homeless sleeping in Turin's doorways gave off that sour smell, dense and peppery, a wall of stench that kept clean people at a distance. They defended themselves by disgusting others. No one wanted to touch them, whether to help or to assault them.

The desire to hide was something Martino could understand himself. He'd already had to slip away in shame when he'd done something mean or really awkward, when he'd been humiliated by other kids or had actually humiliated someone else, driven to flee by his own cruelty.

At the end of his first year, one of his enemies, an obnoxious boy from his old school, had put his arm through the playground fence, picked up a log of dog poo with a leaf to keep his own fingers clean, and thrown it at Martino. It splatted against his jacket and left a mark; even Martino's friends had laughed at him. These days he would have responded by beating him fast and furiously, but at the time he was little, had dog poo on him, and shame took hold of him like a fever with shivers and weakness. He'd crawled into a hedge and hadn't come out during break, when everyone else came out to the playground again to look for him, or when his feet fell asleep. A caretaker had quietly flushed him out and taken him to his lodge, where he put the dirty jacket in a plastic bag and fed him a few segments of mandarin.

Children hide. And children piss themselves. But she was a teacher. The teacher is the opposite of the children: she sits on a platform in front of them and tells them what to do. In fact this teacher had asked him something, and you usually obey the teacher regardless of whether you agree or want to do it. Does a crazy teacher, a dying teacher still count as a teacher? If he didn't betray her, Martino would end up betraying everyone else, everyone who was looking for her. What if she died? It would weigh on him forever. Fear pricked his side, similar to the stitch he'd had a short time earlier, and he wanted to get rid of it. He had a strong urge to enlist the adults and let them deal with it.

Everything that had happened—the girl dying and the teacher going on the run—everything that had fallen on top of him the moment he'd found the hut was too much for him on his own. So why was he in two minds about it? He had never kept a secret like this: he was the only one in the whole village and town, the only one in the world who knew where the teacher was and that she was alive. With that secret nestled inside, it would be impossible for him to get bored, even in Bioglio, so far from his friends. The secret was both a burden and a compensation. It was something he alone could decide. Not his mother or his father. Not the adults.

"You have to tell someone!" he exclaimed.

And yet he continued to stall. He felt torn inside, *I'll tell* and *I won't tell*, back and forth, and he ended up opening the door at home without having decided what to do. When his mother saw how agitated he was and asked, "Has something happened to you?", he instinctively replied, "No, nothing," because that way it felt like he hadn't decided yet, had just put things off.

While he ate his supper he hoped that the teacher had eaten her sandwich and wouldn't die that night. *If she lives, I'll stop copying Piero's homework when we go back to Turin. I'll stop kicking the pigeons, even though I never hit them. I'll stop blowing my nose on my sleeves.*

Later, in bed, he relished the ironed cotton sheets and bounced up and down on the mattress springs. He rubbed his cheeks against the down pillow and felt the woolen blanket. The pillowcase and the sheets were white with blue forget-me-nots on the border, each surrounded by a raised yellow ring in the middle of the corolla.

Martino was safe and dry. He thought he could still detect the smell of the plaster they'd redone the month before, a nice, solid, civilized odor of solvent and brick. He thought of her up there in the woods all by herself, suffering the damp and the dark, and as he fell asleep the woods went back to being the setting for fairy tales: forbidden and dangerous. An ancient, carnivorous place where there are wolves, where children lose their way, are abandoned, and meet ogres and witches. The first labyrinth.

23

SHE TAKES IN THE BOY'S appearance quickly at first. Silvia is not sure it's any different from Giovanna's visits, those of the girls from the boarding school or past versions of herself, all those fleshly spirits that persist in keeping her company. And yet there's a bundle at her feet, a fist-sized packet wrapped in greaseproof paper.

She doesn't feel like opening it. She wants to lose substance, slowly break down like the hut, slough off her body. Her cardigan is almost moss, her skin as cold and white as a grass snake's.

And yet there's nothing of the woods about the packet. It requires her to use her fingers in a gesture from her previous life, touch something that isn't wood, leaf, or earth but comes from a kitchen, maybe a deli. It causes her even more suffering.

She closes her eyes and doesn't open them until night has completed its work. The packet is now difficult to make out, a shadow among many, and it could be a rock. But it's there and suddenly, after much hesitation, Silvia simply picks it up and recognizes the aroma of butter.

A bread roll, a sandwich. Hunger suddenly makes her head spin; she's close to fainting. A violent pain bores between her eyes. The boy wasn't a ghost and he threw her his snack.

If she is to use her teeth to bite, she must coordinate her efforts. Her jaws are misaligned and they can't bite down; gastric juices are eroding her stomach. She gnaws at the crust until she gets to the soft, buttered crumb. Sugar crunches in her mouth.

When she's finished eating, her fuzziness has diminished and she feels guilty. Her fingertips are shiny with butter. *What a nuisance this is.* She needs to vomit, deserves to throw up that sandwich. She pictures her mucous membranes desperately intent on absorbing the food, quickly, quickly before her craziness gets the upper hand, before the nutter in charge decides to put two fingers down her throat.

For the first time, she cries, and behind the dew of her tears she finds Giovanna. She's eating, too: a slice of melon, and she spits the seeds a long way away. Her expression is scornful; at least that's how it seems.

Why did you eat that bread, Silvia? You were doing well, the teacher berates herself.

Oh, how many tales Giovanna tells her, or seems to tell her.

Later that night, Silvia forces herself to remember the boy's face, and she manages to give him a name: Martino Acquadro, from Turin, the asthmatic boy at school. What was he doing up there at the Rovella's summit, a place not even dogs get to? Martino.

A face, a piece of bread, and a few grams of fat have reconnected the teacher with the world. And she's thirsty. Her body is now demanding, wants to be looked after, and she has to hold it at bay once more, start over like a good degenerate mother.

Suddenly she realizes that it's not important because the boy will raise the alarm. Her stomach curdles with anxiety. She wants to escape but she can't move. She strains her ears and waits for them to come and get her, force her to return to the living.

24

THE FUNERAL WAS MOBBED. You had to hold your elbows at your sides just to move and say, "Excuse me," every time. "Excuse me." Giovanna's classmates were gathered in the nave on the left; on the right were her father's colleagues and people who had come down from the valley, their skin tanned by the sun and wind, mustaches yellowed with pipe smoke and hand-rolled cigarettes. Her family sat in the first row, distant and unapproachable, the last outpost of black before the white of the coffin and the wreaths of white lilies.

Anselmo and Luisa came early, while footsteps and whispers still echoed under the vaulting. Luisa settled in a pew at the back while Anselmo stood near the entrance, taking advantage of his height to monitor the stream of people entering. He hoped Silvia was hiding in some cellar or courtyard nearby, under stacks of chestnut wood or under the canvas sheeting protecting tools and machinery. Maybe she had heard about the funeral—there were notices up everywhere and people were talking about it—and would come to say a final farewell. Luisa didn't think so and she was probably right.

"Imagine her coming and being seen by everyone, disrupting things," she said.

Anselmo, however, couldn't sit down and hadn't listened to her. Even so, it was difficult to keep still: something was poking into his kidneys, and instead of jerking around like he wanted to he wiggled his toes inside his shoes, stood on tiptoe, and lowered himself back down on his heels.

From his post he saw Giovanna's mother and father go by, her aunt and uncle and brothers, faces slack with sorrow. Her father swayed to one side as if he'd forgotten how to walk, and Anselmo wondered whether he'd had a mini-stroke. When Sister Annangela came in he started—he was so accustomed to seeing her with Silvia—and the same thing happened with Marilena, who immediately went to sit next to Luisa, putting an arm around her shoulders. Anselmo disapproved when he saw women all made up and wearing lipstick, their eyelashes black with mascara: you don't get dressed up for a funeral. He also disapproved of people who chattered among themselves, no matter how quietly, and when he noticed that Luisa and Marilena were whispering he gave them dirty looks behind their backs, hoping they'd turn around and feel ashamed when confronted with his scowls.

The church was so packed that people could no longer get in and began gathering in the churchyard. The scent of flowers, incense, and melted wax hung over their heads and made him think of the woods, but a fossilized or maybe charred wood, with stumps black like tires. It also reminded him of the lavender and pine poultices their grandmother had placed on him and Silvia to ward off colds, so boiling-hot they practically burned your eyelashes.

"Stay down, Anselmo! Watch how Silvia does it. Put your big head down! Look, if you don't get better you'll have to fend for yourself."

The priest droned on about youth and confusion and from the front row came the sharp sound of suppressed sobbing, as if a dog were whimpering, a shutter creaking. It seemed to Anselmo that it was fluctuating in unison with the people around him, as if they were all flames fluttering in the same gusts of emotion. It hadn't happened to him for a long time, not perhaps since he had gone into the street as a boy to shout out news of the war's end. But then it had been euphoria that brought all those hearts together. It came back to him how, at the time, it was actually Silvia who'd spoken to him about hearts that beat as one and he had poked fun at her expression: "So who are you, Liala, the romantic novelist?!"

He dried his eyes and nose with a handkerchief and began once again peering into dark corners. On the other side of the door a small group looked anxious to disappear: two boys of about thirteen or fourteen with their parents and on their faces mixed expressions of sadness and embarrassment. Anselmo realized that they must have been the friends with whom Giovanna skipped school, those morons. They kept their hands buried in their pockets and every now and then looked over their shoulders, a stupid thing to do since there was only a wall behind them. One of them had a Turin scarf around his neck, maybe the only one he possessed, or perhaps he was too keen on it to leave it off at a time like this. They looked like two whipped dogs and he felt so sorry for them that he waited to catch the eye of at least one boy, to hazard a melancholy smile of the sort that's allowed at funerals. But the boy suddenly hung his head and didn't raise it again.

And meanwhile, Silvia did not arrive. Anselmo didn't give up even after the church emptied. He stayed there for a long time, alone, out of the way, hoping she'd drag herself in later under cover of nightfall.

25

WHEN THE PALE-BLUE CINQUECENTO appeared in the courtyard, the children stopped their ball game and went to inspect it close up, the older kids pushing in front of the younger ones.

"Don't scratch it, okay?" Sister Annangela begged while she adjusted her veil.

There was no lift at the Big House so she had to walk up to the fourth floor. The skylight of glass bricks in the stairwell screened out light, but sounds echoed. A girl, panting, overtook her doing two steps at a time and gripping the banister to give herself a boost, as if stair-climbing were a competitive sport. Sister Annangela heard her turning the key in the lock a floor or two above and a voice asking, "So where have you been?"

"Where do you think I've been? Streetwalking?" the girl replied, slamming the door.

Sister Annangela stood outside Giovanna's apartment to catch her breath before knocking. Giovanna's mother opened it wearing an apron, a dish towel in her hand. She was tall and blond like her daughter, and her smooth, pink cheeks stood out like petals between the creases around her eyes and mouth. Her eyes looked artificial, as if she'd dug them out and replaced them with two pieces of painted ceramic.

"I've been doing the cleaning," she explained.

"Oh I won't come in, don't worry. I only wanted to bring you my condolences and those of the whole school. I couldn't do it yesterday in church."

"There were so many people."

"Yes, so many people wanted to pay their respects."

"Please come in, Sister. Come in. I'll put on some coffee for you."

"Really, I don't want to disturb you."

But Giovanna's mother was already in the kitchen, banging the coffeemaker against the sink to empty it, so Sister Annangela went in and sat down with her. There was a big container of bleach next to the cooker, sponges and steel wool worn with use. At one stage Giovanna's mother got up to put everything back in a cupboard.

"Are those your children downstairs in the courtyard?"

"Yes—the little one is five."

"Then he'll start school next year."

"We're going to send him to the De Amicis on Via Orfanotrofio with his siblings. It's closer, when it comes down to it."

"Of course."

"He asks after his sister. He doesn't really understand."

"What did you tell him?"

"That she went to heaven. That she jumped out of the window and flew up like a bird. He says, 'Well then why doesn't she come down?' I told him she can't anymore and that she's okay." She spoke hurriedly, in great bursts, as if she were afraid of stalling and not starting up again.

"I believe that's actually the case."

"We have to believe it, right? Otherwise I'd have drunk that bleach already," she said with a faintly savage smile. "I feel so sorry for Miss Canepa. Poor thing. She called to tell me not to shout at Giovanna. Poor thing. She's reacted badly. It's not as if she's her mother."

Sister Annangela ignored the note of resentment in her voice—or maybe it was envy because Silvia had disappeared, might be dead and therefore at peace. Envy, too, because Giovanna wasn't Silvia's child, after all.

"How long would she have been in her room?" Giovanna's mother went on. "Maybe five minutes . . . even less. I didn't think about it. I didn't think to open the door again right away. I said to myself, 'Let her calm down.'"

"No one could have imagined it."

"What should I do with her things? I can't stand seeing them around and I can't touch them to put them away either."

"Maybe you should let a little time go by. You don't have to do it now. Or ask someone to help you."

"I'm afraid of taking off her sheets and finding some trace of her, a hair. Did you know she left her slippers on the windowsill? What am I going to do with those slippers now?" She leaned her head back, raised her eyebrows, and swallowed two or three times.

Sister Annangela wondered if she was going to collapse right then and there, and she tried to prepare herself: she seemed on the verge of it but maybe she was like those dangerous buildings that stay upright much longer than expected.

"How is your husband?" she asked.

"He's not speaking, can't sleep. If you ask me, he's hoping he'll have an accident at work to put an end to things."

"Your other children need their parents."

"I know."

The coffee had been ready for a while and it smelled burnt. Giovanna's mother took it off the burner but forgot to pour it out.

"I'll show you something," she said.

Sister Annangela followed her into the room where her children slept in two bunk beds pushed against the wall. There was a single shelf with a few objects on it and a toy box on the floor: a doll, slings, miniature cars. Giovanna's mother pointed to the shelf.

"Miss Canepa gave those books to Giovanna. And that jar." She picked it up. "Three years ago. It's sand from Australia."

The sand was snow-white and fine, luminescent.

"It looks like sugar," Sister Annangela observed. She brought it up close to her glasses. Among the grains she could make out sharp nacreous pieces that must have been shells.

"Do you want it?"

"Oh no, no. Keep it for your youngest. He might like it."

They were interrupted by someone fumbling with the doorknob on the landing.

Both turned their heads quickly, but instead of going to open the door they stayed and listened to the strangled sobs and gurgling. It had to be a horrible prank because it sounded like someone drowning, the ghost of the drowned returning to the family. Giovanna's mother couldn't budge. She sat there, drained and blinking, the cords in her neck tight, her mouth half open. Sister Annangela decided it was up to her to do something.

Giovanna's three brothers stood before her at the door. One had blood running from his nose and was dabbing at it with the hem of his pullover while the other two stood beside him looking sullen. Even they knew they didn't need more trouble. Even the tiniest problem would be too much for the family at that point. With their long fringes and black nails they looked neglected to Sister Annangela, but maybe it was just the end of the day.

"He fell off the wall but it's nothing," the eldest said defensively.

Their mother arrived, wearily reproaching them and taking them to the bathroom where she began to wash them haphazardly. "This was all we needed," she said, not noticing that the boys were upset about it. She was distracted but would occasionally come around, washing and rewashing an earlobe or the ear canal between two fingers with enormous and excessive care. She put two cotton-wool stalactites in the little one's nostrils. The water was still running, so Sister Annangela turned off the tap.

"For fuck's sake, Gino, you look like a vampire," said the middle brother, sizing up the little one.

"Why?"

"A vampire with teeth in its nose. And blood on top instead of at the tip."

"What a creepy comparison," the eldest brother proclaimed.

"What are we going to do now, Nando?" the other two asked.

"Leave me alone for a while." He yawned. In the blink of an eye he'd became the eldest. Giovanna wasn't there anymore to keep them in order.

"Let's play Shanghai," the little one suggested. But from the way the other two rapidly shot him a reproving look, Sister Annangela knew that it must be a game associated with their sister, a game they could no longer play.

She had an idea: she'd ask them to come for a ride in her Cinquecento and she checked with their mother.

"Can I take out the cotton wool first?"

"No, c'mon. Go out like that because it's funny," said the middle brother.

"You'll make the chickens laugh," said Nando.

"Let's take it out, come here. Your name is Gino, am I right?" Sister Annangela stepped in.

"Yes, Gino."

"Nando, Gino, and . . ."

"Alberto."

They went down the stairs. Other tenants were coming and going now and there were strong smells of cooking. Sister Annangela's round eyes swept in front of her toward the tip of her little potato-nose. She was sweating and had to dry her face with her veil.

Once in the car, the boys became animated, asking lots of questions she couldn't answer about the engine, cylinders, and tires. They went to the church of San Cassiano and lit a row of candles. They bought *agnolotti* at the pasta shop in the piazza and on the way back they fished in the sack and ate a few of them raw, dusted with flour.

"Who's paying for these?" asked the eldest boy.

"Oh, don't worry about that. They're on the convent," Sister Annangela replied.

"I found a piece of salami in the filling!" the little one exclaimed.

"No way. It's roast meat inside," Nando contradicted.

"But I can taste it with my teeth. It's saltier."

"It's a bogey that fell in by mistake."

"You mean from the lady in the pasta shop?"

"Yep."

Gino spat his mouthful in his hand and threw it out of the open window while the others jeered and made fun of him.

"Children," said Sister Annangela, since they were expecting it. She made them jump for joy when she turned into the wide opening to the courtyard, barely slowing down.

"But can nuns drive like this?" Gino asked.

"Clearly they can," she said.

26

NO ONE CAME, ONLY THE MICE.

Mice have little girls' faces, and little girls have faces like mice. Mice are running under the leaves, the floor of the hut is a tingling spine, the white moon is a snowy line. Their bare paws make her flesh creep, resembling as they do the minuscule hands of a newborn.

She summons them with the last crumbs of her sandwich, touches their fur with a finger. "Your plaits look like rats' tails," her grandmother would say. "Come and eat something nice. Beans make your hair thick; best of all is an egg yolk. Just think, it can come alive! If you put blood and heat on it, it turns into a chick."

Silvia stopped drinking milk and eating eggs when she grew up.

And now a child has given her something to eat. It's all backward.

The leaves are coming down from the trees, and between the fallen leaves the mice watch her with black eyes, shiny black beads. Pinheads. Suddenly they run. An owl must have flown by. Their fear courses through Silvia, as if she's touched an electric fence.

Marilena the girl slowly approaches, curls rounding the

contours of her colorless face. They're natural but they look perfectly formed, as if with a curling iron. The nuns couldn't tolerate them.

At boarding school, she and Silvia read *Grimm's Fairy Tales* and recognized themselves in the stories of dysfunctional families where mothers might be lost or cruel, fathers useless, and your brothers and sisters your only security. Silvia and Marilena didn't even have those, but they decided to be each other's sister. In fairy tales especially, the dead were alive: their bones sang and could be used as keys. You came and went from the world below. All you had to do was go down a well, walk for a long time, and plump up the pillows and mattress of a witch. Their favorite fairy tale was "The Juniper Tree" because the heroine's name was Marilena, a coincidence that made her tremble with emotion.

The little girl stops in front of Silvia, hands clasped behind her, and starts reciting in the monotone they were meant to use for poems about the Madonna and the angels:

My mother she killed me, my father he ate me
My sister Marilena collected my bones.
In a silk scarf she bound them
In a ditch she laid them,
There where the juniper grows.
Tweet tweet! What a beautiful bird is here!
Tweet tweet! What a beautiful bird is here!

27

THE GAME WAS A SIMPLE ONE: it was war. In class they read a text summarizing *The Iliad* and during the break that followed they quickly divided into groups, the Greeks and the Trojans, without argument. Some aspired to be Greeks—that is, the winners. They wanted to be Greeks like Ulysses and Achilles or like Homer, who wrote the poem and therefore had reason and history on his side. The others wanted to be Trojans—the attacked, those who defended home and country, didn't quarrel, and were super-honorable apart from Paris, the one bad apple. For the children this meant choosing sides between Athena, protector of the Greeks, and Aphrodite, who was aligned with the Trojans.

The Greeks had their camp near the boxwood hedges; the gravel clearing was the Plain of Troy where battles were planned and the Trojans could take refuge behind their wall—in other words the iron fence along the driveway to the gym.

Only the men fought in the war, armed with willow branches stripped of leaves. They lashed arms and legs in sheer warlike violence; it was only blows to the chest that put the enemy out of action. A soldier with a chest wound had to be accompanied to safety by a woman and treated for a defined period of time; after that he could return to battle. With his second wound, however, he had to be treated for longer, and with the third wound he was dead, out of the game for good.

The girls followed the battle with fanatical passion, shouting out any irregularities. The boys' calves and the backs of their hands were streaked with red. They were sweating and trying to organize less chaotic attacks. They'd challenge each other to duels, and then no one could intervene.

Martino and Giulia were both Greeks. With his first wound, Martino turned to see who would be the first to come for him from the camp, but Giulia was already there at his side. Without a word, she grabbed his wrist and dragged him away from the darting blows. She made him lie down and pressed on his ribs with the sleeve she'd pulled over her fist. Silently she counted to one hundred, leaning over to perform her duty. And since she seemed to be so fiercely intent on it and there was no real risk of meeting her gaze, Martino spent that brief minute watching her instead of seeing how the war was going.

Her socks were covered in dirt, her eyelashes were dark halos, and her incisors an adult's, too big for her mouth. He couldn't tell whether the scent of sour apples coming from her was shampoo or warm skin.

"A hundred!" she exclaimed, and Martino sat up at once. Without wasting any more time he threw himself into battle so she wouldn't think he preferred being on the sidelines with her.

He fought with passion since he knew Giulia was watching him—and at the same time he wasn't against the idea of another penalty. He parried and plunged, even when it meant rolling on the ground; little scraps of gravel were embedded in the skin on his knees. He risked having a bad asthma attack but had no intention of sparing himself. He hadn't been so full of joy, so on fire since he'd moved. The second time he was wounded it was Giulia again who looked after him, and it occurred to Martino that her facial features were like those of Pandora Groovesnore, Corto Maltese's beloved.

All too soon, though, the game broke down. With the aid of their helpers, the wounded cheated and went back to war after a few seconds, the dead revived, Ludovico took a lashing to his ear and abandoned camp, and a few of the girls became fed up with cheering them on and went to play hopscotch in the back, leaving the fallen to their fate. The fallen and neglected accused them of treason and suggested the proper wartime punishment: lashings to the backside. The boys cheered as one while the girls threatened to tell the teacher.

Giulia decided they needed an umpire. "We need a Zeus," she said, but at that point everyone was counting on being Zeus, and they started arguing. Because it was her idea Giulia could decide, and she chose Ludovico. The girls who were bored wanted to be goddesses too.

"Oh forget it," Giulia concluded brusquely. "Anyway, break is almost over." She couldn't believe she was so upset by the collapse of that contrived setting in which it was acceptable to touch Martino Acquadro, the prickly new boy.

28

ARMED WITH A LONG POLE, Anselmo followed the course of the Cervo under a cloudy blue sky. He proceeded methodically, cursing himself and the saints as he went along. He hadn't wanted the fire brigade to drag the rivers, despite their insistence, because he wasn't brave enough to confront the possibility that Silvia had followed the girl's example and drowned herself. The night before, though, after the funeral, he'd been alarmed at the thought of pulling up a stranger by sheer chance, someone young and impressionable or some wicked person. He couldn't bear the idea of strangers seeing Silvia bruised and swollen, without her shoes on, say, or her skirt up, eyes white as hard-boiled eggs. If anyone had to face something so awful, that someone should be him.

He pushed his stick into murky creeks and between boulders, where he thought he could detect whirlpools under the water's surface. It was the tense probing of someone who hopes not to find anything. Patches of watercress and water yarrow made his work difficult, and the stream glinted here and there like tinfoil, preventing him from seeing down to the riverbed. A shrew darted between his feet, startling him.

A little farther downstream a few houses clustered around one of the old stone bridges. It was easy to slip there: the flat planes of rocks, smooth and polished, hung over the Cervo like the edge of a gray blanket. Proceeding at a snail's pace, leaning on his stick and making sure he wasn't too obvious—after all, it was lunchtime and people were sitting down to eat —Anselmo heard a voice ring out above the thundering torrent.

"Can't you see that going without food will change your mood?" A cross face appeared at a window just above him. It belonged to an old woman with freshly permed hair. She spotted Anselmo. "Well, what are you doing?"

He wished he could answer bluntly, "I'm looking for my cousin." But instead he said, "Never mind, Signora. It's better that way."

Luckily she didn't make him say it again. She was anxious to talk about herself. Nodding toward the room inside: "Love pangs. She won't eat anymore."

Behind her rose an indignant cry: "Grandma!"

"Oh, Grandma, Grandma," she spluttered. "It's the absolute truth."

"Does she give you trouble?"

The woman agreed wholeheartedly. "Seventeen years old. At her age, I was husking rice near Vercelli, my legs in the water for ten hours and leeches this big. And that one in there"—she lowered her voice to stop her granddaughter from exploding—"can't get a bit of roast meat down."

"They're all spoiled," said Anselmo, who was always reeled in when it came to criticizing youth. Yet that day he was feeling too down, and he was uncomfortable because he knew the woman would be watching him from her window as he fiddled and stirred in the water.

Silvia, Silvia, what have you done to me? When they were children he was the troublemaker, the one who courted disaster and caused problems. Silvia tried to fix things: she secretly brought him something to eat when he was sent to bed without supper and helped him do his homework. Before she went to boarding school, they'd walked to the village school together or had a lift in their grandfather's cart. He recalled mornings when the frost had turned the countryside into a glassy field and they crunched over thousands of tiny frozen needles, Silvia wrapped up warm but still cold, with her usual absent-minded expression.

The two cousins had the same long face, the same close-set blue eyes, identical noses and mouths. If it hadn't been for Anselmo's unusual height, they could have passed for twins. Yet despite all the time they spent walking side by side, eating and drinking elbow to elbow, and sleeping in the same room, Silvia remained a mystery. She'd been incomprehensible even when she was little. A closed book.

Anselmo took his leave of the woman, so anxious to offer him a coffee, and began walking down the Cervo once more. He drew a sigh of relief when the houses and bridge disappeared behind a bend. *Can't you see that going without food will change your mood?* he repeated to himself.

In that spot the slabs of rock thinned out, the shore was all pebbles, and acacias arched over the water, dappled by the light filtering through the foliage. Even though it was well into October, the greenery dominated. He prepared to probe the stretch where the torrent expanded into a spring bordered by large boulders before gushing down beside a waterfall, which was about a meter high and foamy as soapsuds. There were ravines where the water stagnated and a body could get stuck. Anselmo went in up to his calves, felt his boots and woolen socks gripped by icy pincers, the torrent's cold breath on his face. The tip of his stick struck stone, sank into the silt between the aquatic plants.

He was about to get out and thought he'd leave his stick nearby, go back up the bank to a wine bar, when he felt something large but yielding. He had to stop to regain control of his arms; the damned things hung like sausages and had no more strength. His upper body was tense and sore. His mind went to Silvia. If it was her, he'd have to pull her out of there. But he didn't want to prod her with that pike thing. He tried to dig the mass out of the hole between large rocks, working around them; he had to step in closer, plunging right up to mid-thigh. Marbled by light and shifting mud, the water reminded him of a viper's skin and he was disgusted, so much so that he felt like vomiting. Something was tethering the body to the bottom—he was sure now that it was a body. Otherwise, it would have come up; it would be floating.

She wouldn't have filled her pockets with stones.

At last there was a tremor beneath the surface and bubbles shot into the air. Anselmo stepped back. He grabbed the far end of a large torso and a few seconds later, the carcass of a dog. The Cervo's crashing filled his ears again and he realized that though his legs were burning, he could no longer feel his feet.

He hobbled up the riverbank, sat on the dry pebbles, and removed his boots and socks. The dog was slowly rotating before him, a typical sheepdog from the region with a thick white-and-gray pelt.

Anselmo was soaking wet and shaken. He'd have to go back up through the scrub and get his car, then resign himself to letting the fire brigade take care of things with sounding equipment and hooks. He was mesmerized, though, by the dog's corpse, and he stayed to watch it being dragged toward the center of the spring, then down beside the waterfall. At last it gathered speed and disappeared.

29

By the time Martino got off the bus, the wind had cleared the sky and church bells were ringing. On his way home he bumped into Sandra, a heavyset woman who lived in the village. To his indifferent eyes she was identical to all other women her age except that her bosom was really pointy. Sandra still wore those projectile bras that no one had used for at least ten years and Martino had never seen on anyone else.

A trio of older boys were having a go at table football outside the bar. To Martino's surprise, they waited for Sandra to go by and then reacted by smirking, crossing themselves, and rubbing their crotches. Now revved up, they started braying after Martino, "Turin! Oi, Turin!"

He ignored them and quickened his step. He had something else to think about: the teacher he had to get back to, soon, as soon as possible, to see if she was still alive up there. That's what was important. And then, the game this morning and Giulia's proximity, which had stirred his insides, like those chocolates with liqueur centers that make your teeth all dry and then burn your throat (his mother didn't want him to eat them, but his father would say, "Oh, go on, they're antiseptic"). Whenever he thought of Giulia he could feel his gut churning, something sloshing around, almost melting.

He had other things to think about, but as soon as he got home he wanted to ask his mother what was so odd about Sandra that those boys writhed around as they did. Lea wanted to know exactly what he'd seen, and when Martino blushed and remained vague she got some idea. She thought she should leave it there, and another mother might have done so, but she enjoyed feeling that she was different. Sandra's story gave her a chance to teach Martino what hypocrites certain people were, particularly in provincial places like that where a woman who was neither old nor ugly and who lived alone with her asthmatic son was regarded with suspicion.

"Well," she began, "Gianni told me the story. There was a priest who stayed here for a long time, a certain Don Franco. Basically he and Sandra saw a lot of each other." She stopped to allow Martino to take in the information.

He moved slightly, jerking his head backward in surprise. But he didn't say anything, so she continued.

"Sandra never married and was still living with her mother. Whenever her mother was out, Don Franco would come to see her."

"But supposedly priests are not supposed to have anything to do, well, with—"

"With women? No. In theory they shouldn't really get involved." Lea put a box of cornmeal biscuits on the table and sat down across from Martino. Her son was a sprite, skinny and nervous. The more he ate the better. She pushed the box toward him to get him to fish out a biscuit and took up the story again.

"Well, if you ask me it's contrary to nature. Or at least it shouldn't be obligatory. The Church is afraid that love will distract a priest from God and his work. A priest who's married and has a family isn't so willing to move about; he has to tend to practical things like bringing up his children. But Protestants do that, did you know? The Waldensians, too, like the father of that boy Luca from your old class."

"I know who Luca is, Mamma!" Martino was becoming irritated. "I know who he is—I was in the same class for four years." It was the *old class* that touched a nerve.

"Okay, okay, sorry. But it's a fact that Don Franco was in love."

"With Sandra?"

"Why not? Look: it can happen with anyone."

Martino shrugged. The story didn't seem at all exciting to him. This was old people's stuff. And his mother wasn't getting to the point.

"The thing went on for years. They met in secret; their love was forbidden. Obviously, the whole village knew about it. Officially, Don Franco went for coffee and to bless her, but then he'd stay way too long. Still, no one thought there was anything funny about it. Don Franco was a nice man, an excellent parish priest. He was great at football, a mountain of a man, impossible to mark. You could ignore the fact that he had a lover. They pretended nothing was going on. The only one who appeared to be completely in the dark was Sandra's mother. It seems she was a bigoted and overprotective old lady who kept her daughter on a short lead."

"What does that mean?"

"That she controlled her, ordered her around. She kept her from having a life of her own."

"Still, she saw Don Franco."

"But secretly."

His mother's view was important to Martino too. But he was a boy, and he knew that growing up meant forming your own opinions. He knew it because Lea had told him so.

"Then what?"

"Well, one day her mother comes back home earlier than usual and finds Sandra with Don Franco. She has a fit or something like it, goes crazy with embarrassment. To avoid facing the scandal, she runs to the window and throws herself out of it—just like that, impetuously—while the couple stand stock-still, not knowing what to say."

Martino's eyes widened. That was definitely a dramatic turn of events. "Did she die?" he asked.

"Of course not! They only lived on the mezzanine floor."

The two of them laughed and Lea wore her usual clever expression—her ferret face, as Martino's father said. But she was suddenly startled by the similarity between that story and Giovanna's. She regretted not having thought about it earlier and hoped her son wouldn't notice.

"Then why did she throw herself out?" he was asking.

"I don't know. Maybe she lost her mind. Or it was all an act. However, she injured herself in the fall. She moaned and raged against her daughter. People started to arrive. Sandra had rushed out in her slip, and Don Franco looked messy. There was no more pretending it was nothing. He was transferred. Sandra lost her beloved and had to take care of her invalid mother. She's still alive, you know. Only she's lame now and doesn't leave the house."

"Poor Sandra."

"Yes, poor Sandra! In the end, she's the one who was stung. Go figure."

Martino didn't care about this last point.

"Mamma, how is it possible for Sandra to have . . ." Martino pointed to his chest. His cheeks were red.

"You have to complete your sentence, Martino. Why does she have pointy breasts?"

"Yes."

"She uses those cone-shaped bras you can't get anymore. There was a time when they were fashionable."

Who knows whether it was a sort of compensation for Sandra? *Look, I'm a spinster and I've been humiliated but look at my breasts, see how they stick out.* Or maybe Don Franco liked those bras and she couldn't stop wearing them. As a fifteen-year-old, Lea had had one too. She'd put it on and take it off in the darkened doorway, twisting around to get it under her clothes. Her parents would not have liked it.

30

HOW COME PEOPLE HERE *do nothing but jump out of their windows?* Martino thought. *Could it be that the water tastes bad because it's poisoned, and it gradually makes them all crazy?* He looked at the tap suspiciously. *I can't avoid taking a little to the teacher, though. I have no choice*, he said to himself.

He stuffed an aluminium canteen into his schoolbag, a bun, a piece of Gruyère, and a light tartan blanket since there wasn't anything thicker. Lea had washed the floor backward, up to her favorite armchair, and now she was reading with the big mop against the armrest. She wasn't paying much attention to him. All she did was remind him to come home early because his father would be arriving from Turin that evening; it was Friday.

This time he hardly saw the woods. He felt proud of his rescue operation and as he hiked up he convinced himself he wouldn't find her; he grew more worried and increased his pace, even though part of him was almost relieved at the idea. Eventually he became afraid that she might pop up behind him, gaunt and swaying like a zombie. He'd seen posters in Turin for *Night of the Living Dead.*

He was panting when he arrived at the hut. He stood in the doorway and there she was, still leaning against the wall, head drooping, eyes closed. He felt that sudden emptiness you get in your stomach when you miss a step: for a second he thought she was dead but she was breathing. She was asleep. Martino spotted the crumpled sandwich wrapper and let out a silent cheer. She'd eaten it! He decided to leave the blanket, water, and food in plain sight and then sneak off. He knelt to undo the strap on his schoolbag, and when he got back up he met the teacher's eyes. She was no longer a blind dog; she looked more like an extraterrestrial who can't really make out what she's looking at.

Martino didn't know what to say, so he went back to emptying his schoolbag. Tension numbed his fingers. "The bread is a little stale."

"Thank you," she said.

Martino automatically replied, "You're welcome."

Neither dared move more than was strictly necessary.

"Your name is Martino, right?"

"Yes, Miss."

Silvia's face changed, as if she had closed herself off. A few moments later, though, she repeated, "Thank you, Martino," in her hoarse voice.

She couldn't help but stare at the canteen. She'd heard water sloshing inside when the boy placed it on the ground, and the aluminium was pearled with moisture. The roof of her mouth was so dry it felt like it was about to split. Martino must have noticed, since he picked it up and held it out to her, overcoming his obvious reluctance but keeping as much distance between them as he could. Oh, she was grateful to him, now she really was grateful. The canteen was heavy; her arm trembled. She put it in her lap, hoping she'd be able to unscrew the lid—she couldn't ask him to open it for her too. She managed and drank, but couldn't stop a trickle from running down her chin and neck. She wished she were a sponge so she could soak it all up. How marvelous that would be! A simple organism anchored to the seabed, entirely composed of canals, pores, and floating fibers swollen with water, lacking a brain.

Martino had a sudden inspiration. "I could bring you a book if you wanted. My mother has lots of them."

She didn't want him to bring a book. She wanted to be a sponge. And yet once more she replied, "Thank you." The boy nodded seriously. Silvia took in his bony body and angular face, his chin—a little lopsided—his blond hair. At the risk of making him uncomfortable, she continued looking at him because she felt a sort of inner hum lifting. She'd learned that it heralded a breakdown, and she hoped that fixing her eyes on that face, both real and near, would help her to control it. But Martino was already moving out of focus as Giovanna surfaced. She would start gasping in a moment.

"I have to go," said Martino. "My father's coming tonight."

A thud on the roof beams made them both jump.

"A chestnut," Silvia remarked after a moment. She had come back to herself and felt happy about it. The last thing she wanted was to frighten the boy, make him witness some scene.

"I can bring you one of Gianni's books," Martino suggested once more.

"Do you know Gianni?"

"He's friends with my mother."

"Ah, Gianni . . . Gianni." Silvia had not uttered so many words, ones that made sense, for days. It was like walking on a beam. She had managed a stretch without thinking about it too much, but she heard that hum again, felt a sort of dizziness. *Don't do it*, she told herself, meaning: *don't flip out. He's leaving now he's leaving now he's leaving now.*

"Okay, well, I'm going," Martino announced. And since he didn't get any response he added, "I'll be back tomorrow if I can. Is it okay if I come back?"

How long could the boy keep up his story? Sooner or later something would slip out, someone would follow him, or he'd get tired. She hadn't decided whether to go back or not. Yet she'd put out her tongue to drink the rainwater and she'd eaten the sandwich. Even before that, she hadn't managed to throw herself off the bridge.

"Okay."

She listened to his footsteps rustle through the fallen leaves, made it in time to notice a bobble of bottle flies on a wooden knot and to shake the canteen like a talisman, her ears filled with the sloshing. She huddled under the blanket and closed her eyes. Once they were closed, she found herself at home in her messy room.

31

IT WAS A ROOM SHE USED AS A BOX ROOM. She threw into it all the cards she wanted to keep or couldn't get rid of; postcards her father had sent from Switzerland, where he'd worked when she was a girl, for example. They were beautiful: black-and-white views showing peaks towering over squares, cities and small villages, hand-painted scenes depicting young shepherds and shepherdesses in lederhosen and with red cheeks, little goats with barely sprouted horns looking into the eyes of the children who were their friends, and children looking at goats while chewing a blade of grass or whistling.

Silvia had felt mortal rage toward her father, cold and implacable, because he was never there. He'd promise to come for her birthday and then he never did. He left her with her grandparents and the nuns, and in the end he died far away in a work accident. She'd saved all his cards but they were a mess, and mixed up with papers from her students, letters from friends, empty envelopes, lists ticked off.

In the drawers and cupboards of the few pieces of furniture along the walls were stacks of memorial cards, greeting cards, and invitations to Christenings, first Communions, and Confirmations.

On the floor of the room Silvia had piled shoeboxes full of newspaper clippings: former students who'd succeeded at this or that, news about Bioglio (elections, landslides, formal occasions), articles about Jackie Kennedy, Grace Kelly, and Princess Soraya of Iran. There were special editions on Jackie's marriage to Aristotle Onassis and Princess Grace's to Prince Rainier of Monaco, photoshoots with Soraya on holiday in Rapallo.

She'd never probed her own obsession with the three queens (in a certain sense, Jackie was one, too): the widow, the actress, the spurned woman. It must have been something to do with their weddings, the crystal and papier-mâché from which they were fashioned. Grace was the one who irritated her most, in her lavish wardrobe, or standing next to a prince who had cast aside his previous fiancée because she was infertile. Rainier needed heirs and Grace, the great actress, had shrunk herself to enter into that fairy tale in miniature. She gave him children.

Silvia didn't conceal her habit of taking cuttings from glossy magazines—it wasn't a secret passion. Luisa and Gemma kept aside reporting and interviews for her. Sometimes, at the doctor's or her hair salon, she couldn't resist, and she tore out pages and pages from a magazine in the waiting room while the person sitting next to her watched out of the corner of their eye. All that gossip reminded her that even what lies beyond our own horizon exists, and is simultaneously both like and unlike us.

Silvia is in the hut and she is in the messy room. She'd like to turn on the light but the switch isn't working. It clicks in vain and she has to put up with the dim light. There, in the middle, are some of Giovanna's drawings, notes she wrote, photos of her class. Somewhere there's a card with a crooked silvery Christmas tree on it: "Best wishes, Miss Silvia, from Giovanna Morel (and family)." She wants to find it but her hands fall instead on the goats her father sent, the bends in the Rhine at Basel, Jackie in short sleeves and sandals, her grandmother's romance novels. She's struggling to separate the pile of stuff she's already gone through from the rest, but she keeps on looking at the same letters, the same postcards.

She shakes herself in frustration. Her wet clothes feel freezing between her thighs and her waterlogged shoes chill her too. The fog has descended to obscure the woods; the trees farthest away have already disappeared and before long the night's blackout will finish its work of erasure. Giovanna's Christmas tree is invisible, too, and yet it's there somewhere in the forest of her messy room, in the house Silvia has abandoned.

Look what happens when you never keep anything tidy.

The voice in her head could be Luisa's. Silvia is ashamed, and immediately from that shame comes something worse: the nuns. Faced with their abrasive looks she goes back to being a little girl, stubborn, alone, and starved of affection. Like a chestnut plonking onto corrugated iron, a thought strikes her: she never grew up enough. She did it on purpose.

She is Giovanna.

32

LEA SCALDED HERSELF on the edge of the pan in which she was cooking risotto. She poured out the broth with her left hand, sucking the back of her right hand all the while.

"Do me a favor: cut me a slice of potato to put on it," she said to Martino.

A veil of fog had fallen over the window, concealing garden and street. Stefano had arrived a short time before.

"Give me a big hug," he said, turning to his son. He'd say *big* hug and *a brief* moment even though it bothered Lea. Yet he also said *intiero* instead of *intero* and *giuoco* instead of *gioco* and that made her laugh, reminding her of the books she'd read as a child and her school textbook.

Stefano was now standing on a chair in the hallway, where he'd decided to hang a picture he'd brought from their house in Turin. It wasn't a good idea, not least because Martino had gone quiet and his whole body was saying, "That's all we need!" and Stefano was useless at that sort of thing, to the extent that he didn't even know how to hammer a nail in the wall. He couldn't put anything together or repair it; he could barely change a light bulb. On the other hand, he had a few recipes he cooked well: breaded liver, fried mushrooms, stuffed fish cooked in the oven.

"Papa's making something out of solid brick today," they'd say.

Stefano tasted as he cooked and made other people taste, too, and they'd end up already full by the time they sat down at the table.

Lea and Martino appeared in the doorway.

"Don't stand there staring at me."

"Stefano . . ."

"I can manage with a picture."

Martino and Lea moved into the kitchen and listened closely. Soon there was a sound of hammering and crumbling plaster.

"I knew it!" Lea said.

Stefano stopped with his arm in midair, looking incredulous.

"Papa? Papa, you've put a hole in the wall *behind you!*"

"It's not a hole. You can't even see it."

"Sweep up now."

"But this corridor is so narrow—how can I? It should be illegal to build like this."

They laughed, and for a few seconds Martino forgot about his secret and there was no ramshackle hut in the middle of the woods with a teacher inside it to keep alive. Not much later, though, his secret re-emerged at the back of his mind and therefore in reality—beyond the window, the fog, and the trees—and Martino felt once again at odds with himself, observing himself from the outside, too, at an angle, while he ate his risotto and chatted—until going to bed and to sleep seemed like the way to get back inside his own shape. To put himself together again.

*

"So how's he doing?" Stefano asked Lea a little later, while he stood cleaning his teeth in his underwear and she found his pajamas for him, poured his *Idrolitina* in water, hurrying things along so she could get into bed and read.

"Well enough. Managing."

"Has he made any friends?"

"He's angry with us."

"But he's better."

"Yes, and very disappointed about that."

"So no friends."

"He likes Gianni but I'm not sure adults count."

"Oh yes. The writer."

Lea mumbled her agreement, quickly capping the bottle and shaking it to dissolve the *Idrolitina*.

"Now that you know a writer, you'll surely fall in love."

"Oh no. He's not my type."

Stefano saw that she wasn't embarrassed so he knew it was true.

"No trace of the teacher?" he asked.

Lea guessed immediately that she wouldn't be able to read that night, and she felt she'd been a bit simple not to have taken that into account earlier: *you haven't seen your husband for a week, a child is dead, a teacher has disappeared, your son feels displaced, and you want to go to bed and read. What kind of person are you!*

When Martino came home from school upset, Lea had phoned Stefano. Like her, he was skeptical about the possibility of the teacher's returning home safe and sound. Now he was anxious to hear about the search and the girl's funeral as well.

Martino hadn't felt like going to it but Lea had heard that it was well attended. There'd been a picture of the overflowing nave in the paper. Giovanna's father had wanted her to be put in the coffin wearing a white dress, the article had said.

"For goodness' sake. Eleven years old. Holy shit. What does an eleven-year-old know about death?" Stefano muttered.

"Well who knows? Who really knows?"

"C'mon, Lea, don't start philosophizing. A kid jumps from her window. Even just saying it . . ."—he hunched his shoulders—"gives me the shivers."

"We have no idea what goes on in the head of an eleven-year-old. Some little thing, a nothing to you or me, they'll take as the end of the world."

"You can't live like that, though—you yell at your child and they go and throw themselves in the river."

They got under the covers. The sheets were cold and they joined each other in the middle of the bed.

Lea heard Martino snoring in the other room and thought about Giovanna's mother and what she would have to endure, with no respite, until the end of her days. She began crying silently, tears falling from the corners of her eyes and running straight into the shells of her ears.

She dried them angrily with her index fingers and tried to hold back her sobs. She could put up with being a domineering woman or a scornful one, but not a woman who cries. She'd talked about that with Gianni between one break in the conversation and the next, like a mule that plants its feet and bucks—and his analysis: "That's a knotty situation. If you were a character in a book, it would be my duty to unravel it. But since you're a real person, I guess it's up to you."

Fortunately, Stefano made the mistake of consoling her, which gave her the opportunity to take it out on him. She pushed him away and started talking angrily about her pig of an uncle, the one who called her my little redhead, or pretty little thing, and then felt her up. He'd tried to kiss her when she was only eleven, just like the girl, Giovanna, and she'd wriggled away and escaped by running around the big kitchen table—one, two, three times. It was a terrifying, mathematical certainty that he would have caught her sooner or later—but then someone came into the kitchen and her uncle pretended nothing was going on. Lea was so muzzy with fear that she couldn't speak and she'd been sent straight to bed. Sometime later she'd made a huge effort to tell her mother and her mother had told her father. But nothing happened. Her father and her lecherous uncle continued to go fishing together. Her father would come home pleased with his bucket of trout and perch, and it was Lea's job to clean them; she opened their stomachs and threw out the guts, doggedly scraping off scales over which the light threw miniature rainbows.

"And it's not that they didn't believe me, you see. They knew themselves that he was a predator, a kiddie-fiddler. This is what goes on at home. What do we know about that girl?"

"Okay, I'm sorry. But calm down."

"Listen: good night. I'm going to read a couple of pages—if I don't, I won't be able to go to sleep."

Her eyes glued to her book, Lea asked herself if a lot of what happened later hadn't been a response to her parents' betrayal, parents who hadn't lifted a finger to help her. *I'll defend myself, I'll give the orders, I'll decide when to let my pants down.* The trigger? Her predatory uncle. But no, people aren't that simple. Who knows where it came from, her feisty character, what combination of genes, conversations, and events had shaped it? And choices, she said to calm herself. Above all, choices.

33

"Let's have a kickaround," Stefano suggested to Martino, and that's how they spent the morning.

Stefano was a tennis instructor at the Press Club in Santa Rita and had been a promising skier. Slow to the point of being lazy, he wasn't focused on finishing first but on doing things right. His bread and butter had been the slalom, the most technical of descents, and he excelled at it thanks to perfect tracking; he enjoyed the work of his muscles and tendons, the pull of skis that wanted to swerve, the plumes of powder behind him.

"You've got what it takes," his instructor told him, smoothing sunscreen as thick as white lead over his nose. "What you lack is the competitive mentality." And during training he'd yell, "Move that behind, Acquadro, shift it! Push! Push!"

When he was about fifteen Stefano had stopped racing entirely. He wasn't interested in competing, a trait that would turn out to be useful in his relationship with Lea. On the weekend he preferred being with girls to being on the slopes.

Having an asthmatic child didn't make him nostalgic for trekking, long swims, or athletic feats. He never badgered Martino like his father had him.

His father was fanatical about mountaineering and their house had been plastered with photographs of him on rope climbs, at the summit, embarking on a *via ferrata*, resembling a tiny black insect in a line on a glassy glacier, secured to walls of gneiss or granite, wearing knee-length socks and a cabled woolen jumper, ice-axe and cable hooked to his backpack, lips white with cocoa butter. He'd made Stefano follow him through the same scenery and they, too, had taken a few photos, but for Stefano they had always been inhospitable spaces where he was engaged in a pointless struggle: demonstrating to his father that he was man enough. At eighteen, Stefano had switched from skiing—still a mountain sport—to tennis, which his family considered a hobby for the pretentious, for spoiled brats.

Asthma wasn't actually incompatible with physical effort. You just had to go slowly. That morning, Stefano realized that Martino had more stamina than usual. He kicked freely and didn't hold his side or pant when he stopped. Stefano ruffled his hair. "This air is good for you, Mouse. Look how well you're playing!"

Martino cracked a faint smile, but soon found a way to make matters clear. "I want to go home."

"Let's do this: next Wednesday, you and Mamma come to me—take the train."

He both wanted to and didn't want to. Going back to Turin for the weekend would mean he got to spend two days in his room but as a guest, with empty spaces for the things he'd taken with him. Seeing his friends, who might have gotten used to being without him—and finally sitting through the journey in reverse, from city to forest, his heart shriveling as it had when they came to Bioglio for the first time and it felt as though it was wilting inside his chest, kilometer after kilometer. He'd thought of the mummies in the Egyptian Museum, their skin turned to leather, and also of the prunes wrapped in Speck that his mother baked in the oven.

"I want to go home and stay there," he clarified.

"Ratìn . . ."

Martino kicked the ball against the wall of the house so forcefully that the rebound threatened to come straight for him and he made a very undignified leap to dodge it.

Stefano looked at him to see if there was scope for downplaying the situation. There wasn't.

In that black mood, Martino remembered the teacher who was keeping him there worrying—shuttling back and forth with things to eat and drink—and he poured his discontent out on her. He was this close to telling his father about her.

"Let's do something nice this afternoon. Come on, there's that monastery between farms that we wanted to visit. Your mother says the church is Romanesque."

The secret made his tongue tingle.

"Would you like that?"

I'd like to off-load the teacher, and make myself look good for having discovered her. I'd like to get out of here and go to Piero's house until I can convince you to let me stay in Turin.

"On the way back we'll get some hot chocolate."

Martino made up his mind. Blabbing about it, no: that wouldn't be honorable. He'd go up there to the teacher one more time and tell her he didn't feel like continuing to . . . what? Cover for her. Bring her food and water. She'd have to make do.

"Hey! What's the matter with you?"

"That's okay, that thing—the monastery."

"Come on then, let's get washed up."

Martino continued to mull things over. What if the teacher had vanished in retaliation? He would look like a moron. A traitor. Double traitor. Like someone who'd betrayed the teacher and everyone else. Even if something awful had happened, it would be his fault. *Why didn't you say something right away, Martino?* He didn't know why. Because he was so surprised. Unsettled. What had his mother said? "Moral dilemma." But also for a bit of adventure. Because he was bored, because he was sad, because he was angry with his parents and wanted to keep something from them. Now, though, he felt impatient, fed up, and he knew the time had come to put a stop to it.

34

THE FIRST TIME someone saw Silvia they believed it.

She was in Santhià and had asked for information about the regional trains for Milan. A little while later the man selling tickets remembered the teacher. He'd seen her photo in the papers: a woman of medium height, chestnut-colored hair and blue eyes, whom he'd never met before. She hadn't taken the train so she must still be in the city.

Anselmo and Luisa arrived barely an hour after the call. The ticket seller found the newspaper and pointed triumphantly to the photo. "Looks just like her! As far as I'm concerned, it was her."

"Was she okay?" asked Luisa. "It's been four days since she disappeared."

"She was okay. Fine."

Luisa and Anselmo looked at each other. *Someone's helped her without saying anything*, he was thinking resentfully. But Luisa's hopes were fading: it was unlikely that Silvia looked "fine" after what had happened.

They scoured streets, cafés, and shops. Anselmo ahead, raving. He'd burst through the doors, bells would tinkle, and he'd be gone already. He used to do the same when he played hide-and-seek with his cousin as a child: he opened all the doors and in his excitement he missed things. Concealed in wardrobes, behind curtains or under the bed, Silvia got away. So he forced himself to slow down a little. In the meantime, Luisa was pounding the side streets. People turned their heads to look at them. "Have you lost a child?" worried a woman loaded with shopping bags.

Luisa was breathless and heard a clattering in her head. Suddenly she thought she spotted a figure at the end of the road who might be Silvia. Anselmo had gone into another café and she didn't want to waste her chance by going back to tell him. She picked up her pace without losing sight of the figure, and actually focused on her with such intensity that two figures appeared before her eyes.

The woman was dressed in black with the right hair and the right walk, dragging her feet a little. No handbag. When she turned the corner Luisa began to run, her own bag bouncing back and forth like a swing—she felt an urge to drop it, but she didn't. She called, "Silvia!" and her voice sounded hoarse. There was no one else in the street, only doors and gates and a stretch of stubbly grass on the opposite side, garages with their doors pulled down. A dog on a balcony began barking, going in and out of her field of vision, as anxious as she was.

Luisa tried to focus on the shoes. Low-heeled leather loafers. Dark blue or black? Silvia's were black and these looked blue, or black faded by dust.

No. They really were blue. She let the race come to an end.

The woman stopped at the entrance to a house and took a bundle of keys from the pocket of her coat. Only then did she turn around, affronted.

A few steps away and as red as a tomato, Luisa had her handbag strap wound around her wrist and she held it tight in her fist. Her hair comb was hanging from an ear. She leaned against the wall and apologized, explaining that she'd mistaken her for someone else, someone she'd been looking for for days. The woman had been afraid of the racing behind her but now she was angry about it.

"Fine, but you can't really follow people like that!" she said in a Milanese accent.

"I'm very sorry. The worry . . . I made a mistake."

She went back to Anselmo, who'd become angry in the meantime because he'd lost sight of her.

"I mixed her up with someone else."

"Good going! Did you at least ask if she was the one at the station?"

Luisa hadn't thought to do so. "But she definitely had a Milanese accent. If you ask me, she's the one the ticket seller spoke to."

"If you ask me, if you ask me." Anselmo lost it. "And according to you, can we settle for that?"

So they crisscrossed the whole village, barely exchanging a word, and afterward they retrieved their car and combed the streets, cutting through the rice fields. The combine machines had already passed through, harvesting the small plants, and stubble was being burned in many plots, leaving the fields with the black and yellow stripes of a tiger's pelt. Even with the windows closed Luisa could still smell diesel and manure.

"I knew immediately that it was no use trusting that cretin at the station," Anselmo mumbled, and she let him run with it.

"We were naïve," she admitted.

"But I don't know how you managed to mistake a Milanese woman for Silvia."

He gave her a slap on the knee before changing gear, and Luisa thought that by dint of acting crazy and running away, Silvia had forced her to stay and be normal forever, as long as her natural life should last. She turned toward the countryside. The Alpine slopes were the same blue as the sky, and you could make them out only because of their peaks, jagged, stony, and snow-white against the misty white of the clouds. Pale-gray herons hunted along the canals, the watery surface doubling them like figures on a deck of cards, one sharply outlined, the other grainy yet sparkling. Luisa spotted a heronry between the black locust trees, dozens and dozens of large nests where other birds stood waiting.

35

AT FIRST, even Gemma had felt hopeful about it. Later that evening, she could have slapped herself for being so stupid.

She'd tried to keep herself busy while Luisa and Anselmo were out, turning the mattresses and beating the rugs until Corrado emerged from his cabin made out of two chairs and a quilt. They'd told him Silvia was traveling and now he wanted to know where, exactly, and if she'd gone to see the kangaroos and koalas again. To keep him calm, Gemma told him one of the war stories he liked, with a happy ending.

"The Italian army was defeated at Caporetto, remember?"

Corrado nodded uncertainly.

"It was dangerous to remain here, so we escaped. We had to cross the bridge over the Tagliamento, but they blew it up to stop the enemy. My mother, my siblings, and I got across but my father was left on the other side because he had the caleche and cows and was going slowly."

The Bridge of Delights, they called it, and a crowd of soldiers and refugees were passing over it along with lorries and wagons, donkeys and mules. Gemma heard the explosion behind her, sensed the air quivering with heat. Then came ear-piercing screams that could be heard over the roar of the raging river. She saw red, granular splotches of sludge on the soft mud. A child said, “Look! It’s like jam,” and his mother slapped the back of his head to shut him up and then immediately held him tight.

In Ferrara, where they were evacuated, Gemma came down with Spanish flu. She was one of the few to survive among the many sick people crushed together in rooms shared by different families. But her hair came out in clumps and the skin on her hands and feet peeled off. To console her they told her she was molting like snakes and cicadas and she would surely survive because plants, too, lose their leaves in the autumn, only to be reborn in the spring. A string of more or less inspired reassurances. Fourteen-year-old Gemma, though, was horrified by her half-bald head. She felt the sparse strands and despaired, retorting that snakes and cicadas were disgusting: she preferred horses with manes and dogs with thick, curly fur. She peeled off layers of dead skin and threw them in the brazier to annoy everyone with the nauseating stench of grilled fly.

She didn’t tell Corrado that bit, but she told him about walking down the road weeks later, a handkerchief around her neck, and recognizing her father, who’d managed to make it to the city and was asking for information in a *latteria*. The sight of his red mustache through a filthy window haloed by the sun was still, for her, the picture of happiness. When he entered, the bell on the door rang like the blast of a trumpet. She threw herself at him, into his first embrace: the two of them, alone, without any claims from her siblings or her mother. She took him all the way to the overcrowded apartment and that evening she let him shave off the rest of her hair and call her "my little boy."

The story over, Gemma began to regret her optimism, because that's how life was and you had to accept it: there was a time when she ran into her father during the debacle of world war, and there was a time when Luisa and Anselmo failed to find Silvia in the village of Santhià.

36

Martino couldn't justify going out by himself before Sunday afternoon, after almost two days of strict monitoring during which Lea and Stefano had tried to understand how he really was; or rather, how bad his mood was, though they didn't come to a clear conclusion. They asked him what he did in the woods.

"Nothing," he replied.

"If you want, we can go for a walk together sometime and look for mushrooms. There'll be a lot of them."

"I prefer playing Sandokan."

"Ah, okay. Well . . ."

"Maybe you can go with Crivelli's son. Wait—what's his name?"

"Maybe next time."

"What direction do you take?"

"Depends. To the little chapel."

Lea looked at him questioningly.

"Halfway up."

"Be careful not to twist your ankle."

Before going to the woods he filched a piece of cake, the tag end of a salami, and a couple of apples. Leaves were falling off their branches and the first stars were peeking out of the sky. Invisible birds and lizards rummaged through leaves on the ground. Maybe he should have hidden, too, in Turin, on a building site or in Valentino Park at night. They'd have found him right away, though: in a city, there are people everywhere.

When he got to the hut Martino remembered the promise he'd made to the teacher last time: to bring a book. He'd forgotten, and for a moment he felt like a failure, but he quickly told himself that he was there for the last time, to put things straight. And yet . . . it was pointless to deny it. He had hesitated; he'd had second thoughts. He was on tenterhooks, and he tried to calm down by repeating his prepared speech. *I'm sorry, Miss, I can't go on keeping quiet. Everyone is looking for you and they're all worried. I'm sorry, Miss, I can't go on keeping quiet. Everyone is looking for you and they're all worried. I'm sorry . . .*

So as not to frighten her, he knocked on the beams and waited a few seconds before peeping in.

She was sitting down and looked more composed, more *normal.* Martino couldn't have said how, but it was the impression she gave, as if her shoulders and arms were in a fairly controlled position, her hands and feet still but not lifeless, not askew. Her face, though, looked terrible: white and green, like a piece of Gorgonzola.

"*Ciao,*" she greeted him.

"Hello."

"Don't you feel well?"

It was absurd to be questioned by someone who was more dead than alive. Someone getting by on his leftovers, whose voice sounded like it was coming from the catacombs.

*

For at least a day and a half, Silvia had been forcing herself to focus on the boy and construct some kind of logic. Meanwhile her mind kept filling up with Giovanna and other old things she thought she'd buried for good: her thoughts, heaped and incoherent like the cuttings and postcards in her messy room. She couldn't get on top of them. She knew, though, that she had asked too much of the boy and would have to tell him. She had to free herself of that unexpected anchor. She'd tried to train herself, but every word cost her tremendous effort and sounded odd: an unused tool, a broken washing machine thrown out in the woods. *Martino, I apologize. I asked you to do something difficult, something wrong. It's not fair for you to feel responsible for me. Don't come back. I promise that I will return—if I feel like it. When I feel like it, I'll return. As soon as I feel like it. But don't you worry.*

Nonsense. The goose was cooked. The boy surely felt responsible and guilty and she felt guilty about him too. Guilt on top of guilt on top of guilt. They'd been hand in glove from the moment he'd turned up there. Silvia hadn't succeeded in disappearing. Again she wondered if desperation might encourage her to do away with herself. *But you're eating, you're drinking!* a hateful voice accused.

"I brought you some cake but I forgot the book," Martino said.

"Doesn't matter."

He cleared his throat but the teacher beat him to it.

"I'd like to tell you something."

"Yes?"

"I need to apologize."

Martino hoped that she wanted to be rescued, that it was all over. *Give me free rein now and I'll tell my mother. Then we can phone your family.*

"I asked you to do something difficult. It's not—something wrong, yes. It's not fair for you to feel responsible for me. Don't come back. I promise that as soon as I feel like it, I'll return. And if I don't feel like it, it's not your fault. It's . . . something I've decided. It's to do with me."

"But if I don't come, who will bring you something to eat?" Martino objected.

Silvia didn't know what to say.

"And what if you're too weak to walk?"

All the objections she'd put to herself he was now directing at her. He felt betrayed, and doubly so. The teacher was asking him to continue keeping quiet, but without his being able to keep an eye on her. *No, my dear. Nope.*

"What if you need something and there's no one to help you? Or if there's a cold night?"

It was a stalemate.

"You're right," she admitted.

"So why don't you go back home?"

She mumbled, "I can't. I just can't do it."

Martino then remembered that essentially she was half mad or she'd gone crazy, so clearly you couldn't really discuss everything. It was, as they say, a minefield. He felt a kind of calm. It was up to him. He had to keep a steady nerve, like the privateer Yanez de Gomera. The teacher was getting better. Maybe he just needed to be patient. Make a proper campsite, bring her some more blankets in the meantime. She really was behaving like a child, hiding because of her shame and grief, and he told himself that she would inevitably come out of her den at some point. He'd have to help her get there. And maybe she wouldn't end up in an institution either, as Gianni feared.

"I'll keep coming so you'll get better faster." Martino let himself get carried away with his recent resolution. He didn't want to threaten her; he wanted to save her. "Otherwise I'll tell."

He sat for a while, looking at the tips of his shoes and wondering if he had accidentally gone overboard.

"Did your father come?" the teacher said, as if she hadn't even heard his blackmail.

She really was strange.

"Yes, but how did you know about my father?"

"You told me about him last time."

"Oh. Well, he's leaving right after supper."

"My father didn't live with me either when I was your age."

"How come?"

"He worked in Switzerland. I missed him, I think. I was rather angry with him." So where had that come from? Starvation, an unhinged voice that didn't even sound like hers, the fact that she was distracted by the thought of the cake he'd mentioned at the beginning.

"Papa misses me," Martino admitted. "But I have my mother here."

"I lived with my grandparents."

"What about your mother? Was she gone too?"

"Um, you know . . . my mother. She was . . . she died young. That's it."

It seemed as if the teacher wanted to apologize for sharing something depressing, but on the other hand he had the impression that they were taking a few steps forward and he was relieved. Was it so surprising, he thought, that the pain of losing your mother as a child would make you more liable to end up crazy and alone in the woods? What would he be like without his mother? A disaster, a complete disaster! He didn't dare go too far into the specifics just then. But in his brain he heard the terrifying word *orphan*, a prerequisite for changes of fortune. The teacher was a sort of overgrown Oliver Twist. And yet, he reflected, being brought up by your grandparents had to be better than getting lumbered with a wicked stepmother, sent to an orphanage or the slums of London.

"You lived here in the village, right?" he asked, just to say something.

"Yes. The house near the fountain. The one with wisteria climbing the wall."

"We have wisteria in our courtyard."

"Well I never."

"The house was all musty inside." Lea had said so, holding her nose. "That's why we had to replaster."

"Did you help?"

"I did the whole corridor by myself."

Silvia noticed that she'd made headway. She could hold some sort of conversation almost without being aware of it. While one part of her brain registered the ascent of a small bird, a treecreeper, on the trunk of the beech tree and its disappearance behind the shelf of bark where it had surely built a nest, her other thoughts kept whirling around Giovanna, Giovanna, Giovanna. She was speaking like a robot, but more or less managing to follow the rules of conversation.

"The other night, though, my father was trying to put a picture up and he hit the wall with the hammer—the wall behind him!" Martino lit up as he imitated his father's gesture, and Silvia managed a crooked smile.

"He completely ruined the paint. Oh well, I'll fix it later," the boy said, boasting a little.

Sitting there in front of him, Silvia hadn't yet eaten. The wrappers and a new bottle of water sat on the ground, but she was ashamed to put food in her mouth with her hands, with her chin hanging over her knees like a monkey. Being watched while she ate was like admitting that she was giving in to her body's survival. What is suffering when you're faced with a slice of cake?

Incontinent Canepa, Greedy Canepa: the nuns again. I've never dealt with those damned nuns.

And to think that even she couldn't get down the slop they served in boarding school: she'd toss it surreptitiously into a metal box so that during break she could bury the whole thing under a yew tree in a remote spot in the playground.

The boy seemed alarmed once more. Perhaps he'd been gone too long. So Silvia asked him what she usually asked children. "How's school going?"

She was referring to his marks, or to how they were getting on without her.

Martino didn't understand. "Okay," he said haltingly.

"It's difficult to change schools," the teacher added, resurrecting another emotional tangle: the school, twenty years of students. *Silvia, you're all in a muddle,* Marilena's voice had said. As long as the other voice couldn't make itself heard, the one that wanted her dead. Or rather, wanted to humiliate her because she wasn't dead. *Mortify*, according to the etymology. Here they are again, here are the nuns, the great mortifiers.

Silvia, stay where you are. Don't get lost, it urged. *Listen: the boy is talking to you.*

" . . . my first teacher in Turin, but she wasn't very good. The second one was, though, especially explaining math and science. I had lots of friends in my class. I'll be with them again in middle school, with my best friends," Martino was telling her.

"Oh, you will?"

"We're going back to Turin next year. We're not staying here. As soon as my asthma gets better."

"And how is it?"

"Better, a lot better."

They told each other something else of no consequence: she made signs of approval, mostly, to ensure that she didn't make a mistake. Before he left, Martino took the empty canteen so he could bring it back full the next day.

Silvia allowed herself to be mesmerized by the treecreeper's comings and goings. The little bird hopped up and up the trunk, its feet gripping the bark and never missing, its tucked-in head making it appear even more focused. After a short while she realized that there were two of them spiraling up the beech tree. Even in the dusk their feathers seemed tipped with gold.

37

THERE'S A STORY, and it harks back to the time before her birth. It seems that even the spiders know it, the crows and the treecreeper couple. She reads it in the branches poking through holes in the hut, in the sooty mold that covers some of the leaves like a felt hat, and in the few forgotten or decayed objects—spade, billhook, rake—with their shadowy corollas.

More than once she's heard the voice of her grandmother, busy with something else as she always was: mending, sweeping, cooking, sharpening knives, plucking a hen. Silvia's great-grandmother was working in exactly the same way in the other half of the house. It was Silvia who asked, "Why don't you speak to each other? Why do you pretend that Great-grandmother doesn't exist? Tell me again." And her grandmother would give her a dirty look. There were plenty of reasons—it was obvious—but the official silence had begun with the zabaglione.

Her grandmother had had three children: Anselmo's mother, Silvia's mother, and another girl, and the third girl was blond with a small nose like a beak. She came down with meningitis and was very ill. Grandmother wanted to make a zabaglione to make her feel better, but her mother-in-law was against it. She was a hard, pitiless woman with an acid voice.

"That's not necessary. It's only a fever. You spoil the child!" she said. "We can use those eggs for lunch tomorrow. Someone will surely come. My son will bring us some devil of a socialist, you'll see." Grandmother gave in, but the baby died during the night. She hadn't given her any zabaglione for fear of an argument, but from that moment on she stopped talking to her mother-in-law.

Silvia couldn't comprehend how she had managed to impose upon her grandfather and convince him to erect a wall that divided the house in half, rendering the floor plan impossible and forcing them to build a staircase on the outer wall as well as wooden walkways enabling them to get from one floor to another. Grandmother shrugged. "I told him, 'I won't look your mother in the face anymore. I'd rather leave.' And it was true: I was furious. Most of all with myself."

From the moment her daughter had become ill, Grandmother became obsessed with feeding her. It had been a mistake to go along with the refusal of the zabaglione but she'd done it for a quiet life, out of weakness, knowing deep down that she should have insisted and shut her mother-in-law up, beating the egg yolks with a spoon until they turned lighter, barely dented with sugar, and put it in her baby's bird's mouth, filled her tummy with a simple, uncooked dessert. Luckily at the time she still had her other daughters, Delia and Albina. And later, when she'd lost Delia, too, Silvia had been left in her care, for her to raise. That's exactly what she said.

"But my aunt was dying anyway," Silvia had objected as a girl.

"Yes, she surely would have died regardless."

"Even if she'd eaten the zabaglionc."

"Even if she'd eaten the zabaglione," Grandmother repeated wearily.

Now Silvia remembers her grandmother's impulse to stuff her with food, spreading a lump of butter on her bread, slipping shelled hazelnuts into her pocket like ransom money, and her own need to binge and then starve herself for entire days afterward, as if to drive her grandmother crazy. During those years Anselmo was often in the house as well, but he would eat and that was that. He'd eat everything without raising his face from his plate, and then he'd go to his disowned great-grandmother and get the same again.

38

On Monday Lea booked a visit to the optician in Biella. For weeks it had seemed as if her sight was deteriorating and she had a headache—like toothpicks behind her eyeballs—that she was convinced was related to her blurred vision. Over the years her mother had become so shortsighted that she recognized people chiefly by the sound of their voices and Lea was afraid of ending up like her, a half-blind mole bumping into door frames. The optician said, though, that her sight had not deteriorated much and he gave her a discount on some frames because they looked so good on her. They were leaf-shaped, with tips pointing toward her temples.

"So you don't think I seem like a mole?" she asked.

"No, I really wouldn't say that." The bald-headed old optician was surprised.

She went to wait for Martino in the café near his school, ordered a coffee at the bar, and had a chat with the barista: Turin, Biella, a nod toward the tragedy. No, her son wasn't one of the girl's classmates, the girl who—the girl, anyway.

A young man with a brand-new leather briefcase came in and

the barista whispered to her that he was standing in for Canepa; he grimaced as if to say *I don't envy him.*

Lea decided to introduce herself. She wanted to know how things were going at school, what the atmosphere was like given that it was so hard to get anything out of Martino. The substitute teacher had a black beard and deep-set half-moon eyes. His eyes were as black as his beard and they shone like the tourmaline in a bracelet Lea had had years before—who knew where it was now.

In the space of a few minutes Lea noticed that her gestures had lost all their spontaneity: putting her cup down (she made it clatter too loudly on the saucer); smoothing her hair behind her ears (she did it too slowly). After a busy morning, her lipstick had bled and she felt sticky little clumps of it at the corners of her mouth. She had an urge to lick them, or else scrape them off with her incisors and swallow them. She tried wiping them off with a napkin and asked for another glass of water.

Clearly for the first time, the teacher found himself substituting for someone whose whereabouts were unknown—and on top of that, in a class upset by the loss of a classmate. He confessed that he found it horrible and extremely difficult. Yet as he did so, he turned on Lea a look both absorbed and cheerful, and she noticed it bouncing between her hair, eyebrows, and lashes, moving down from her forehead to her coat collar (actually very high-necked). They weren't keeping an eye on the time, nor were they paying attention to the children outside walking on the pavement. Lea nearly threw away the receipt for her new spectacles with the dirty napkin.

As she went past the large window of the café, Sister Annangela noticed Greppi, the substitute teacher, with the mother of the new boy, Martino Acquadro, Year 6C. She'd run into her only once at the beginning of the year, but her red hair made her unmissable. There was nothing wrong there. They'd met, had a coffee together. But Sister Annangela was very observant, and she noticed Lea smiling and tilting her head to one side while she stood on one leg, teasing a heel with the tip of her other shoe. Meanwhile, with one elbow on the bar, he leaned toward her as if he were sitting in a box at the theater intent on enjoying the spectacle. And Sister Annangela guessed that the story wouldn't end there.

39

THAT AFTERNOON Martino was wheezing when he arrived at the summit of the Rovella. It was the fault of those three boys who shouted at him and made fun of him because he was new in Bioglio and spoke with a different accent, which they mangled. Or they'd make farting sounds, palms under their armpits, when he walked past. If they weren't at the café playing table football, they were sitting on the cement embankment smoking. They'd hold their cigarette butts between thumb and index finger and then send them splashing a long way out. They talked about arses that made the rounds and boobs that sent them cross-eyed, just to be heard.

His mother went to work to make up the time she'd lost that morning. Martino had stuffed himself and then set out through the forest, starting at every noise, imagining those three idiots jumping out of the undergrowth. Once he got to the top he found Silvia staring into space again, catatonic, her eyes looking boiled. She wasn't expecting him.

"Miss?" He tried to go along with her and looked in the same direction, toward the wall of the hut, where there was only blue lichen resembling miniature heads of lettuce and damp cracks.

He took his time putting his paper bag on the ground; inside was a long loaf of bread and an edition of his favorite comic series, *The History of the West in Color.*

He'd thought about it long and hard because he wasn't sure the Dakota warriors' raids were the right sort of reading for the teacher, but he didn't want to go through his mother's books; she'd notice for sure. He'd chosen the issue with "The Legend of Sitting Bull." Everyone likes Sitting Bull, of course, and there was the part that made him shiver, when the witch doctor goes to the future Big Chief: "Now I understand that your long slumber wasn't due to illness, but the Great Spirit wanted it! He has put his mark on you. If you speak to him, he will listen!" Too bad Silvia didn't seem in any condition to read.

"Miss?"

"Anselmo?" she asked.

"It's Martino."

She didn't open her mouth and, feeling let down and frightened, Martino got ready to go. But he hadn't walked twenty meters before a strangled roar stopped him short. Farther down, between trees and piles of dry leaves, he could make out a furry mass: a wild boar. It wasn't snuffling, nose to the ground. Its glittering eyes darted here and there until they alighted on him.

Martino had heard grisly tales of wild boars that savaged dogs and tore old women to pieces. He backed up slowly, with a weight on his chest that boded ill. His fingers tightened around the inhaler but he didn't take it out of his pocket for fear of dropping it and losing it in the undergrowth. The boar lifted its bagpipe of a nose and sniffed the air. Martino was now close to the hut and he called out: "Miss, Miss! There's a wild boar!", his voice so altered that it unnerved him.

Just then the boar bucked and took off, head lowered, hoofs galloping rapidly despite the ascent. Martino was about to leap to one side when the teacher came out of the hut holding the blanket. She got in front of him and twirled the blanket in front of the boar, which slowed down and traced a small circle, snorting. Martino watched it moving the tip of its snout up and down, up and down like a rubber hose.

"Get out of here! Go away!" the teacher said. When she decided the beast was tamed, she grabbed Martino by the sleeve and drew him into the hut.

He sat down, breath whistling, took out his inhaler, and opened his mouth to breathe in the spray.

"Are you okay?"

He nodded to let her know he was all right and she went back to her corner as if she wasn't expecting anything else. Martino's nose stung with the smell of ammonia the teacher's movements had released.

"But why, why did it charge?"

"It didn't charge."

"But—"

"Blustering. A young male. Wild boars only charge in desperation."

Martino was getting his breath back. It seemed that the sounds of grunting and of leaves being stomped were fading away.

"Gone," the teacher confirmed. She was definitely more present than before. She'd gotten up, reacted in a hurry, and she'd rescued him. But something was keeping them apart.

"Who is Anselmo?"

"Anselmo?"

"You called me that, before."

"Oh! My cousin. Are you really okay?"

He nodded again.

"Sorry. You know, I have certain thoughts every now and then"—Silvia touched her stringy hair—"which act like glue."

"That's okay."

"When I was your age, everyone was always telling me I had my head in the clouds."

"They tell me I'm fidgety and don't know how to stay still."

"I knew a girl like you at boarding school. We're still friends."

"You were at boarding school?"

"Yes. With the nuns. To learn."

"Couldn't you just go to school?"

"There was a war on, and curfew. And anyway I couldn't have taken the teaching diploma here in the village."

Martino wanted to hear about the boarding school. Every so often his maternal grandparents would say to him, "If you misbehave we'll send you to boarding school," and he had in mind the institute where the storybook rascal Gian Burrasca ends up. He expected it to be like a prison for boys where you eat dirty dishwater. And now, finally, he knew someone who had been there, and he asked her to tell him about it so eagerly that Silvia didn't feel she could let him down. She talked about the stink of turnips and rat poison and about the discipline. She told him how they had to keep their eyes lowered when they went out for walks so as not to meet a man's eyes. She told him there wasn't much food and it was often disgusting, and she talked about the bowls of milk they drank to add calories to their meals. Since she'd left, she had in fact stopped drinking milk. She couldn't stand it anymore.

"Was the food that awful?"

"It made you vomit," she confirmed. "Sometimes we'd hide it in the biscuit boxes and then throw it away."

"And what if they'd found out?"

"They'd have punished us. We had to eat what we had, even if it tasted spoiled."

"And what were the nuns like? I mean, with you."

"It depends. We liked Sister Elvira. She taught us science in the playground with earthworms, seeds, and roots. In general, though, they were very strict. Everything had to work perfectly, without hiccups. Crying was a problem, getting angry, arguing . . . Ugh! Better not argue. Breaking something, making it dirty, getting sick. Being afraid."

"Were you there for long?"

"Seven years."

"Seven years!"

"Middle school and high school. To get my teaching diploma."

"And you never went home?"

"Yes, of course. At Christmas, Easter, in the summer."

"Not that often," Martino commented.

"Some of them were always there. The-Ones-With-No-Families, we called them. But my grandparents came to see me almost every Sunday in the dray cart."

Martino's curiosity was insatiable, but the teacher was tired. Her face looked torn, as if her features had slackened little by little, and her stories, too, became less restrained.

"We called one of the nuns The Mastiff because of her saggy cheeks and pug nose. She beat us hard. I remember how her knuckles were black and blue when she wielded the cane. One of The-Ones-With-No-Families, Agnese, would spit on the plates when it was her turn to serve the table. I loved her for that and we became friends."

"Was she the fidgety one?"

"No, that was another one."

"And did you?"

"What do you mean?"

"Did you rebel?"

"Not on your life. I've always been a scaredy-cat. But at least I wasn't a snitch."

"Some of them were?"

"Some, yes. Agnese spent entire nights on her knees beside her bed as a punishment."

Silvia didn't tell him that once, when the nuns were exasperated, they'd given the girls tranquilizers and Agnese had turned into a sort of calf, wobbling on her feet and looking around with eyes narrowed to a slit, as if the sun were shining in her face.

"However, I wasn't doing at all well myself. I was clumsy, absent-minded, and greedy for the sweets my grandparents brought me. I didn't know how to cook or sew. I worked hard at my lessons but I never was one of the best."

"But if you're a teacher?"

A strange laugh escaped her. "You hardly have to be top of the class."

Martino thought she was saying it out of modesty.

"So you were happy when you left," he concluded.

"Yes. I didn't know how things would go outside, but I had a job so I couldn't complain. My friends—above all, I was sorry for my friends."

"But you were always together there, in the same city."

"Most of us. But you know, from living together, one goes . . ."

A yellow light thick as broth poured over them through holes in the roof between the corrugated tiling and the beams. Martino got to his feet.

"Well, you know what it's like. You, too, have friends in Turin who are far away."

"For a year."

Silvia wondered if he was exaggerating the length of time or trying to minimize it.

"If they don't forget me," Martino added.

"They won't, for sure."

"How do you know?"

"Experience. And hopefully you'll go and see them before the year goes by."

"My friend Ago, Agostino, is like Agnese."

Agostino fought with the older boys and knew how to stand up to anyone, even adults. Once when he was defending a cat, he got hit in the mouth with a stone that broke his front tooth.

"I wish I could be like that," the teacher admitted.

"Me too."

Silvia was on the verge of remembering why she'd chosen to be a teacher, other than convenience and habit: because of the restlessness of children, their fears and intelligence, because of how instinctively tender they are even if they are too new, too mocking and courageous to understand pity; because of the way they look when they're learning something, before they become people pressing ahead, like newborn animals whose arrival in the world is a miracle, a wonder, until at some stage they become simply cattle as far as we are concerned.

"My fidgety friend is someone you know," she revealed. "It's Sister Annangela."

"Sister Annangela!"

"After boarding school, she was the only one to take vows."

Martino took in the news. Silvia and Annangela in uniform, being caned. He peered outside, but it didn't look like there was anything big moving around.

"What do I do about the boar?"

"Nothing. Don't worry about going back down."

"But he attacked me!"

"He didn't. I'm telling you he didn't. Go home. If you see one, don't run. If you need to, take the long way around."

Martino stalled in the doorway, but as soon as he made up his mind he left at a brisk pace, looking left and right as he did before crossing a road.

Nothing would happen to him. Silvia hadn't thought about the fact that for an asthmatic, fear itself is a danger, even if it's unprovoked or disproportionate. She let herself be drawn back to the age of eighteen: a girl like so many others, undermined by the humiliation that spared no one at boarding school—after all, it was an established educational technique—but one who didn't like feeling sorry for herself. Thus, a little humiliated, a little proud, she had prepared for adult life.

40

MARTINO AND GIANNI were waiting for Lea to finish adding cheese to the polenta. There was something about her that was difficult to put a finger on, something confusing. Still, she was behaving as usual: quick, almost brusque. She opened a window to air the kitchen, which was hot because of the cooker.

"You're shining like polished silver tonight. What's gotten into you?" asked Gianni.

"Don't make me laugh."

"Really, Lea, you haven't had a little tipple while you've been cooking?"

"No, but I'd love one now."

Gianni poured her some red wine, a drop for Martino, too, just enough to wet his lips. It seemed horribly sour to him—tongue-curling—and he immediately ate a piece of cheese to chase it down. He decided they wouldn't be suspicious if he tried to talk about Silvia. They'd never imagine him capable of playing a double game like a secret agent.

"In your opinion, if someone runs away and hides and doesn't come out, are they crazy?"

"Are you thinking about the teacher?"

"Yes," he admitted. He must not have been very subtle.

Gianni took him seriously. He said he couldn't speak as a doctor, a psychiatrist, only as someone who observed people and read books. Madness, in his view, wasn't something that existed outside people of sound mind, but as a possibility within each of us.

"Maybe that's why it makes us uneasy. When we're extremely sad, disappointed, frightened, or angry," he said, "we may step into it. The possibility can become reality for a minute, weeks, sometimes years. There are things that really scramble your brain: losing someone you love or being mistreated as a child. Some of us can withstand the blows and some can't. I know people, for example, who have sunk into great sadness. It's called depression. They literally don't eat or get out of bed. Are they ill? Are they crazy? That's not important: the most important thing is to understand whether they want help and how they want it. Of course, there are also more serious, more obvious cases. Where it's easy to say: crazy. People who are convinced that they're Napoleon reincarnated, who slap themselves, or cut off two fingers with an axe like Guerino, that old man, just because he was ordered to do so by the voice of his father, who'd been dead for twenty years."

"Who? That old guy carried around by a donkey?" asked Lea.

"That's the one."

"But someone who hides . . ." Martino took it up again.

"Martino, it's best to be honest," his mother interrupted.

"What's most likely is that the teacher put an end to her life. That she's not coming back." She ran her fingers through his hair. "These are tough things, I know. I know, Ratìn."

Martino looked at Gianni, who held his palms up as if to say: anything is possible. But he looked blank.

41

THE BUILDING was from the late 1950s and stood in the San Paolo area. Its balconies were cluttered with clotheshorses, plastic deck chairs, small tables, tricycles, geraniums, stacked plant pots, rugs, and blankets left out to air, all partially hidden by striped awnings that had faded in the sunlight.

Luisa and Giulia spotted the entryphone panel. Names, handwritten, had been added in at different points and taped over more than once.

"There it is: Belletti."

A tabby cat came to rub against Giulia's socks but her mother pulled her along. "Come on. We mustn't make them wait for us."

The walls of the apartment were papered in bottle-green, hazelnut, and mustard-yellow. Belletti's wife had already put the coffee on and she brought it straight through into the dining room, a smallish space with nothing in it apart from the round table in the middle. She opened up a games table with a green cloth surface and set the plastic tray on it with cups and a glass of lukewarm orange squash. Giulia had a tummy ache and tried not to look at Signor Belletti, who was making small talk with her mother and explaining that he preferred to be called a clairvoyant. The man was balding, with a chest that had expanded over the years, an enormous head, and eyes that were magnified by glasses. His smooth, fleshy cheeks and bulging forehead made him seem like an elderly infant, as if his hair had not yet grown in and his head and body had never been in proportion.

It was her friends from the factory who'd advised Luisa to see the clairvoyant. Two of them had visited him personally and could vouch for his being a very serious and humble person, a council employee who in his spare time exercised his gift in the service of others.

"Trying doesn't cost anything," they'd said, "or, well—the price is reasonable."

Luisa's faith was accommodating. She believed in what were called presences, in guardian angels, dreams that foretold the future. Actually, she did feel the conflict between Catholic teaching and her attempt to contact the other world after she'd forked out the money, but in her view the Church didn't manage to encompass all the relationships between the human and the divine, though it definitely covered the majority. In situations of extreme anxiety, trying everything was forgivable. She drank her coffee, staving off impatience. Giulia looked over at her nose and thought: *Why didn't I get my mother's nose? So straight. I don't look at all like her.* She'd insisted on being taken there and was sure that Luisa wouldn't have given in if she hadn't been strung out with insomnia and false hope.

There had been other sightings after Santhià. Anselmo had taken a leave of absence from work so he would be ready to run anywhere along with the fire department or friends already retired.

Gemma and Luisa cooked at home while they waited, telling themselves it was better to remain pessimistic. Meanwhile they cleaned floors on their hands and knees, attacked tile joints with a brush, or applied themselves to the blinds and rugs to dispel some of their anxiety. Whenever they heard the key turn in the lock, they held back from running down the hallway. Anselmo would come in by himself, tired and enraged, drink a glass of water and baking soda in the kitchen. He found the blinds half washed and arabesqued with trickles of black water, rugs rolled up, the furnishings in disarray, and he whined. They let him do it, knowing that it was his way of pouring out his desperation, the way they did by scrubbing and polishing. To each his own.

Signor Belletti sat down and his wife left the room, closing the door. A crucifix hung on the wall behind him, above it an olive branch with dusty leaves. Luisa held out a photo of Silvia, which he turned upside down on the table before closing his eyes to concentrate.

Giulia struggled to believe it would all be useful. She'd heard that clairvoyance, like prayer, works only if you truly expect it to, and she didn't want to sabotage Signor Belletti's abilities with her doubts. She closed her eyes, too, and when she opened them again Luisa was moving the tray to a chair and the man was spreading a large map of the area on the table. He took a pendulum from a drawer, a brass cone hanging from a thin chain, and let it fall perpendicular to the map.

The chain quivered. Belletti slowly moved it from side to side, over the city, hills, and the surrounding mountains, valleys, woods, and villages. Luisa seemed troubled and Giulia realized that she feared the total absence of a sign, which would mean that Silvia had gone a long way away or, worse, that she was dead. She gripped the hem of her skirt in her fists. Imperturbable, Belletti moved his arm. He was passing over the city again when the cone began to rotate. His hand looked motionless and relaxed while the pendulum turned and turned.

"Clockwise," he commented. When he moved the chain to another area, the twisting slowed until it stopped, and when he went back over the city it regained momentum.

Belletti put the pendulum down and turned the photo of Silvia over. Giulia had goose bumps and the hair on her arms was standing straight up.

"According to what I'm seeing, your relative is alive somewhere in the city. I can't be certain, but I believe she's hiding in a church."

"A church?"

"Behind the organ, maybe, or in one of the back rooms."

Luisa was worried. "She won't have been able to drink if she's been indoors."

"Maybe she's drunk the holy water, Mamma!" Giulia suggested earnestly.

Belletti nodded in approval with his massive head. "You can continue to hope. And as for holy water, I stock up every year with water from Lourdes. Let's close with a nice blessing, okay?"

From a drawer he took a small perfume bottle bearing a sticker with LOURDES on it in capitals. He sprayed the map, the pendulum, and, quickly, his two guests.

42

THE CALL OF THE BARN OWL sounds like her alarm clock, and Silvia gets up and goes out of the hut. The plants are breathing; humidity is rising from the soil.

"My feet are cold," she used to say to Anselmo when they went looking for mushrooms, and he'd reply, "Think about the animals—they're always outside, but we'll soon be going back to the stove." Once, they burned their heels on the red-hot, cast-iron stove, trying to warm up in a hurry. They often burned themselves on the embers and sparks from the chimney or matches they lit to burn ticks. Silvia would dig them out of their dog's skin with alcohol and tweezers and Anselmo applied the flame. Swollen with blood, they looked like green olives or mature acorns and before long they'd burst, making the hens squawk as they scratched around, hoping to eat.

Silvia breathes into the frozen bowl of her hands and thinks that each morning in the woods is a triumph. Being damaged is the same as being alive. The damage you've suffered is proof of your existence: the parasites, mold, scratches, ulcers, loose teeth, matted fur, maimed wings, lameness. There's nothing undamaged apart from an embryo (sometimes), a hard, closed bud, a spore. She, dirty and hungry, is nothing special.

Anselmo: she wants to remember what he was like when he was Giovanna's age. A large, awkward boy, a bottomless well who could devour entire loaves of bread and half a dozen raw eggs, sucking them directly from a small hole in the shell. Report card day: hers average, almost good, Anselmo's disastrous—a report that incited turmoil, punishment, and running away.

In the woods, Anselmo hurled stones at the crows with a slingshot, always missing, and peed from treetops with his friends. They'd play in the village, throwing lumps of coal at each other and giving the mule slices of bread dipped in wine for the fun of seeing him sway. At night they'd scare their grandmother, howling under her bedroom window until Grandfather came out holding a broom. Then it was the German occupation, and Anselmo didn't understand any of it, but he argued with everyone.

Spring of '44, on the Biella–Oropa tram, a couple of months before the partisans of the Bixio battalion took the valley. The carriage stopped and Germans and fascists looking for deserters, real or suspected, sifted through the passengers while the lorry waited, engine running, before the extended colonnades of the sanctuary.

Anselmo hadn't bothered to bring any ID with him. Not yet fourteen, he was taller than the carriage and his hooked nose made him look older. There was nothing in him that inspired compassion or suggested his age. They chose him: he stood there blinking in a row of adult men, thin and white as a leek.

Silvia feels once more the rush of heat that hit her face as it does when you bend over to open the oven door—and again she sees herself going over to the republican and pointing, with a faintly apologetic smile: "That idiot, my cousin—if only he hadn't grown so big. He's thirteen years old. You can check, but right now I'm going to take him home. Can't you see how alike we are? Can't you see that he doesn't have a single whisker? What are you trying to do, shoot a child? He'd be perfectly useless if you did make him work in Germany. In fact he'd be a pain."

Afterward they walked all the way down to Biella. Silvia tried to keep up with Anselmo, who was striding through the meadows and scratching his arms till they bled. The light was dazzling and the wide valley, spread before them, seemed bewitched by silence. To release tension, they threw pine cones at each other and the last coarse lumps of snow. Farther down they pulled up clumps of sorrel, sucking on the acidic stems veined with red.

"But it's not true that I'm a pain," Anselmo grumbled. Just then he tripped and fell into a hole and laughed till he cried.

The present seeps into her memory and Silvia feels something of Anselmo's anger and the fear he must feel for her. But she can't bear it, so she turns her thoughts to other anxieties, the everyday ones that don't concern her.

Anselmo lives in a constant state of overexcitement, and being so close to him means almost feeling the anguish humming in his chest like a hornet. He doesn't want his children to run, jump on the sofa, or knock into furniture because he instantly imagines them in the hospital. They mustn't be out of his sight for long or away from his supervision. They can't go on swings, can't sweat, drink from fountains, eat prosciutto or cheese without bread. According to him, these are grave threats to their health and good manners and he treats them as such, shouting like crazy and threatening punishment. He can't bear it when Giulia reads for a long time, for fear that she'll ruin her sight, and yet he wants her to be top of her class. He never allows her to read at the table, and that rule would be reasonable were it not for the fact that he dines with *La Stampa* open in front of him, using the water jug or vinegar bottle as a stand, and grumbles whenever someone moves it to pour a drink or season their food.

Anselmo lives in constant fear of something terrible happening. And yet, for all his ranting, no one is afraid of him, and when they obey him it's out of exasperation more than anything else.

Now Silvia has given him a valid reason for being afraid, and has united the family in the same fear.

Once again she dismisses the idea, seeking other images in which to take refuge: Marilena (but she brings boarding school along with her), the house in Bioglio (Anselmo comes back forcefully), Giulia. She might be able to calm down thanks to Giulia—if only she didn't come as a pair with Giovanna.

Sudden gusts stir the foliage. The woods have become once more an alliance into which Silvia has intruded: trees that change color without knowing it, animals without peace and without sin. A family of roe deer are sitting on their haunches among the cyclamen in the small glade, but when one of them scents her presence and pricks up its ears, the others rise in unison and flee as fast as they can.

43

AT SCHOOL, the children would end up talking about Giovanna before their first class or during break, in small groups and in low voices.

"Maybe she leaned out too far."

"She was angry and lost control of her movements."

"She didn't realize."

"If you ask me, she did it on purpose."

Once Ludovico asked, "What if she regretted it while she was falling?"

They shivered. Giulia said, "Well, it didn't last long," with an echo from her friend Angela, "Yes, five seconds if that."

"So you're saying that's not enough time to regret it?" Ludovico sought reassurance.

But it was, which was why no one answered.

Martino burbled something about her maybe having been courting danger, the way you do when you're riding your bike and you feel like closing your eyes to see if you can keep your balance.

"Who would do something so stupid?" Angela frowned.

There were a few scattered giggles.

Martino tucked his chin into his neck and crossed his arms. Let them laugh, he thought, but he felt hurt and a little ashamed. At least he'd stopped himself in time, before revealing that two summers previously he'd broken his wrist doing just that—riding a bike with his eyes closed. The accident had been very painful, but he'd made his entrance at school the next day with a fresh plaster cast on show and laughed about the exploit with his friends in a way that seemed completely different to the squawking of the Biellesi children. Like a hero who, disdaining danger, or rather inviting it, must reckon with the consequences of his audacity. He'd kept his cast. It was on the top shelf in his room in Turin.

44

By this time Martino had a favorite route for climbing up to see Silvia. It was simple, almost a straight line. He'd go out of his garden at the back, cross the lane, and follow a faint path, a rocky, weedy track that cut across the side of the hill. His shoes sank into succulent turf and glided over patches of cyclamen.

When he got halfway he came across a bush he considered a friendly presence; he didn't know its name, dogwood, but he liked the leaves, which were changing from green to steak-red. After that he had to cross a stream, jumping across on the rocks, and a little after that the small chapel rose up beside a yew tree loaded with fuchsia-colored berries. From that point on the vegetation began to change: a spruce grove, then thickets of sorb, juniper, hazel, ivy-clad acacias, pale globes of mistletoe hanging from bare branches, intertwining leaves, intricate grafting, and bundles of dead branches fallen on top of each other. It was the wood in its primordial state of arboreal confusion and reciprocal suffocation.

On Wednesday, Martino got to the dogwood and plucked off a leaf—it looked like a flame, especially when he twirled the stalk between his thumb and index finger. He got back on track, and because he was looking around as he walked for fear of running into another wild boar, he didn't notice the furry shape he almost stepped on until the last moment.

He was too much of a townie to know what it was with any certainty: weasel, stone marten, ferret, or pine marten. The animal was lying on its side on a bed of clover, its back arched, paws together. The chestnut fur was still pretty, and a yellow patch expanded over its throat. Its whiskers barely quivered in the air, or maybe it was Martino's breath that stirred them as he crouched down to get a better look. Small, sharp teeth and an edge of pink-and-black gum stuck out of its mouth; curved claws crowned its paws. It wasn't clear whether it had been killed by a hidden gash, a bullet, or distemper.

Once he got up there, Martino asked Silvia if it was a good idea to bring Gianni's dog with him on the pretext of taking it for a walk, so that it would scent animals and defend him. But she replied that if there's one way to annoy animals it's to bring a dog around and, what's more, Gianni's griffon was old, and since it had had a stroke it couldn't even run in a straight line.

They talked about dogs. Martino wished he could have one, but Lea didn't offer him any hope. Silvia's grandfather had kept a female pointer, white and orange and devoted to her mother, Delia, who had fed it the edge of her piecrusts when she was a girl. The bitch's offspring were still populating the village with bastard hunting dogs. They talked about mothers, and Martino got more worked up than he had envisioned. His mother was likeable, he said, she made him laugh and she knew a lot; sure, she sometimes got agitated and his father would say, "You're a piece of work," which usually made the situation worse. You had to let her read in peace, not dirty the floors with your muddy shoes, not drip everywhere when you got out of the bath, not eat while you were walking around the house, not get into bed with your clothes on—stuff like that. But other than that she was really nice; played cards, talked to him about books for grown-ups like *Jane Eyre* (he cleared his voice and moved on, because it contained a delicate discussion of a madwoman in the attic and, who knows, maybe Silvia had read it herself). And as far as he knew, she was the only mother with red hair and freckles all the way down to the backs of her hands.

Silvia listened, gentleness showing through the exhaustion on her face. She barely remembered her mother; Silvia hadn't turned five when she died. She'd once read a magazine story about a woman who'd lost her father; he must have been famous but she no longer remembered who it was. For the funeral speech, the daughter wanted to talk about his great passion for woodworking, and since she didn't remember how he'd gotten started she phoned to ask him. Only at that moment, with the receiver next to her ear, did she realize that her father could not be reached: he was dead, and she would never be able to speak to him again.

In her own case, Silvia didn't know very well what she had lost, let alone who her mother was. No one had helped her to reconstruct it and when she got to the age of reason she hadn't wanted to think too much about it. She was nostalgic for someone she didn't know and for a relationship she hadn't had, and also she mourned the person she might have been had her mother brought her up.

"I barely remember her. At some point I must have asked, 'Where is my mother?' They must have said something in reply. 'Your mother has gone to heaven, she *had to go* to heaven.'"

"In heaven? With whom?"

"'With the angels. With God.' I think I was jealous of God, who got to spend time with my mother while I didn't."

Other memories: tearing the wings and feet off insects, asking for them to be fixed, hearing that it wasn't possible, it was too late; you can't fix a grasshopper's leg—the wing won't move. Believing that your mother watches over you (like God, with God) and feeling uncomfortable about that, inadequate, a humble spectacle. They said it to comfort her: "Your mother is still watching you from above." Silvia aimed embarrassed smiles at the heavens. There was a period when she was ashamed to go to the loo, and she'd hold it in until her bladder was so stretched it hurt and her intestines threatened to rebel. One evening after prayer she decided to address a frank request to her mother's soul: *Please don't ever look at me when I'm in the loo!*

"Do you know," she said to Martino, "it feels strange to be older than my mother ever got to be."

Silvia had two portraits of Delia. Who knows what pictures she would have invented without them? In one photo with scalloped edges Delia was holding Silvia, less than a year old and all lace, in her arms, supporting her firmly, hands under her armpits and chin grazing her fine hair. For Silvia, that photo was proof of her being in love—the only proof, in the absence of memory, of the only reciprocal falling in love she'd experienced in her entire life; it portrayed the most intimate contact she'd ever had. She would occasionally ask herself whether she had perhaps remained loyal to her mother by not starting her own family and embalming the orphan she'd been somewhere inside herself. Such thoughts made her feel profoundly uncomfortable.

To Martino she repeated the commonplaces of family lore: Delia of the swanlike neck; the fingers of a pianist; a lover of animals. According to these attributes, her mother was different not only from her, her daughter, but also from her parents and their world, their social class; or maybe she hadn't had time to get old and become like her family. Indeed, her grandfather had been a distinguished man, and it was said that as a young woman her grandmother had had a nice figure.

After Martino was gone, Silvia went on talking by herself as she hadn't dared to with a ten-year-old boy. With the passing of time, she'd noticed her friends becoming intolerant of their own mothers, critical and drained. She knew that some of those older mothers were sources of unhappiness and torment, and she forced herself to consider that things could have turned out like that for her: it wasn't certain that she and Delia would have had a good relationship.

On the other hand, boarding school had been full of orphans who'd had it much worse than she had, with no one to love or care about them. *Don't go on about it, Silvia—you're hardly the only one.* People around her got sick and died, there was Mussolini and then the war. Her own grandmother had spurned her mother-in-law after the death of her baby girl, but without making a scene:

her mourning had taken concrete form, as silent belligerence and walls erected to divide the house. When she referred (a rare event) to the death of her daughters, her grandmother called them "my calamities, the first and the second."

With few exceptions, among them Gianni, those who'd been in the army, who'd been demobilized, the Alpine troopers who'd come back from Russia with fingers eaten away by the cold, draft dodgers, those in the resistance, people who'd been consumed by hunger in the concentration camps, who had escaped the bombs, pulling their children out of bed and huddling in cellars—all these people she knew were fleeing from the story of their own pain, forever varying the same ritual catchphrases: "I've seen things I wouldn't wish on anyone," "I've seen things that can't be repeated," "The things I've seen will go with me to the grave."

But through not going on about it, you've gone crazy. Look: look at the state you're in.

The teacher fell silent because once more it struck her internally: the conviction that the one sure way of not going on about it would be to end it all. The usual spiteful whisper was quick to suggest: *But you survived. You survived your mother and you survived Giovanna.*

She crawled around, found the billhook, and, in an act of rebellion, brandished it against the voice.

Despite everything they did, the nuns never had a single student who committed suicide, but you *did!* the voice accused, not at all impressed.

45

MARTINO HURRIED toward the village, disturbed by the teacher's story.

Her mother had vanished from one day to the next, but how did she know she hadn't gone away on purpose? That she'd ceased to exist and was to be found nowhere on earth? He imagined Silvia looking for her mother and the arms of her grandmother replacing those of her mother, and then himself not hugging his mother, whose red hair always ended up in his eyes or even in his mouth, but his maternal grandmother.

Maybe her grandparents had taken little Silvia to the cemetery, in which case she must have seen the coffin lowered into the ground, or at least the tombstone with her mother's photo in an oval frame. Once awakened, he couldn't get that morbid daydream out of his head, and he kept on walking without paying attention. He passed the dogwood and found himself about a dozen meters from someone facing the other way.

The boys from the café were there. He hid behind a bush, seized by suffocating anxiety. They'd catch up with him and tear him apart, the idiots. Where did they think they were going? Did they know about Silvia's hut? He forced himself to stare at something small and close to calm down, but all that red in his eyes wasn't helping—it was an exciting color, a warning color. Those three, though, weren't moving, or rather they weren't walking in any particular direction and, oddly, they weren't speaking either.

Martino saw their elbows shaking vigorously, as when Lea was whisking egg whites and it made her whole back quiver. Now and again one of them would let out a grunt or gulp some air and hold it in his chest. They'd stuck a page torn out of a newspaper to a tree trunk, showing a shape, a woman in a bikini posing as a mermaid on a rock.

Martino finally noticed that the three boys were looking from the photo back to their loosened trousers where their willies were hanging free. He'd have done better to take that chance to scurry off, but he was riveted by the spectacle of their joint masturbation. He was still too young for erections, nocturnal emissions, and a broken voice, but he knew something about it all anyway. He guessed, for example, that the kisses between Corto Maltese and Sandokan weren't the end of their amorous adventures and that sleeping wasn't the only thing adults did in bed.

One of the boys yelped as he stopped squeezing himself and bent forward to avoid spunking on his shoes. He wiped his fingers on the moss, on his socks. *Get away without being seen or heard*, Martino decided. But the boy, the one with the horse's face and a tuft of flattened hair on one side, began recovering from his trance and looking around to be sure no one was about to surprise them. Martino made the leaves crackle, jumped and stumbled, and the other boy reassembled the fragments behind the dogwood until they came into focus.

"Hey you, what are you doing here? Are you here to spy on us?" He looked as scandalized as a priest.

"What's going on?" another one echoed.

"Turin followed us."

"I did not," he defended himself.

"Turin!" thundered the one who seemed to be the leader. He stood in front of Martino, legs spread, black curls stuck to his forehead with sweat.

"Torino likes salami, guys. He likes bechamel sauce. You wanna try it, right?"

The other two laughed coarsely.

"His mother taught him. Even though she's married she always invites someone else to supper. Does everyone do that in Turin?"

"Gianni is our relative," Martino explained, but they ignored him.

"It's disgusting! With that cleft he looks like he's got an arse on his chin," the third one butted in.

The Leader contradicted him. "Leave it—I'd do her."

"Fuck off," Martino burst out.

The Leader opened his eyes theatrically and turned to Tufty. "Bring him over here."

"I have asthma! I have asthma! You can't. I'll die!" Martino panted, and while they dithered the memory of Silvia twirling the blanket to confuse the wild boar flashed before him. Instantly he remembered the dead creature under the dogwood. He turned and it was still there, a scrap of fur lying on clover, tiny fangs, yellow chinstrap, pink gums, and now a few flies too. Overcoming his repulsion, he grabbed its tail and felt the tiny bones under its fur. He whirled it once to gain momentum and then threw it toward the Leader, shouting, "Watch out, it bites!"

The Leader staggered backward and ended up with his bottom flat on the ground. The carcass landed on his legs only a whisker away from his open fly. The other two stared speechless with disgust, but Martino was already flying down the slope, nearly twisting his ankle with every step, scattering twigs and leaves on all sides. Wisely, he stifled a victorious smile.

46

ONE EVENING fifteen years earlier, Silvia was sitting in Marilena's garden. They were young and Marilena's first child was sleeping in the pram, the white bonnet knotted under his chin making him look like a little pilot. In the orchard on the opposite side of the wide bend a female roe deer slunk between the plants, bending her head to graze upon fallen apples and turning her downy hindquarters to them. Marilena's husband had just finished the watering and was coiling the plastic hosepipe.

Marilena picked up the knife. "I'll cut you another slice of *gâteau*." She liked using French words—she said *pardon*, *dommage*, *en plein air*—and Silvia saw her husband shaking his head in the distance. She almost never refused an offer of food. "Give me a big slice," she said, and when she leaned forward to hold out the plate, her chair knocked against the wrought-iron table.

"None of it is true," Marilena let out at one point, as if she were pursuing a conversation that had already started and was clear to the two of them.

"None of what?" Icing sugar and greasy crumbs were raining all over Silvia's jumper but she didn't notice.

"None of what they told us at boarding school. All that stuff. This thing's sinful, that one's wicked."

"I know."

"I want to tell you something now." Marilena lowered her voice and moved her pale face closer to Silvia. "My husband, you know"—and she motioned toward him with her chin—"well, you know he's very hairy. You saw him with his shirt off while he was cutting the grass. The first night we were married, after everything that was supposed to happen happened, he falls asleep and I go to the bathroom to wash. I put on the light and I see myself in the mirror with curly black hair all over me: my stomach, my bosom . . . I was scared for a second and I thought: *Look, Marilena, this is your punishment for being with a man!* As if they'd grown on me, right? Divine punishment. Which makes not a particle of sense, given that we were already married. But it upset me anyway, and I couldn't help but see Sister Slumpy with her wonky ear and hear her threats all over again."

"God is watching you!" Silvia chanted in a high-pitched voice.

Marilena fluttered a hand over her chest and Silvia finally brushed off the crumbs.

"They really overdid it."

"But it was a weight on us! It was like being a hunchback carrying a really heavy rucksack," Marilena huffed. "I thought it was part of me and I couldn't get rid of it. Feeling guilty for being happy, for example. When Slumpy told us that Jesus never laughs in the Gospels—if anything, he cries. Well even if he happened to laugh and it wasn't written down, you can be sure he wouldn't have cracked up like we did, our mouths open so wide you could see our tongues."

Silvia gestured as if to say: water under the bridge. During that period she was convinced she'd put everything behind her.

"So it's not because of the nuns that you didn't get married?"

"No, I don't think so. I don't think I felt like it."

"Well I did want to, but I didn't get married just to get married. You remember how I always used to say, 'Saint Anna the Blessed, may I soon be wedded!'"

Silvia put a hand on Marilena's arm in her somewhat mechanical way. She knew it was true. Marilena loved to talk about whatever was going through her head (the story of the hair—no one else she knew would have brought up something like that). Not Silvia, and she would never let on that she hadn't had sex with a man or with herself, if you discounted a few rare, clumsy, and inconclusive blunders. Nor would she ever talk about the letters she'd exchanged with the doctor who had operated on her grandmother when she broke her hip and was bedridden for months.

Hidden in the woods, though, Silvia remembered a dream about a boy from Bioglio. She must have been Giovanna's age and she liked him. She was conscious of it at the time because she responded to his presence as she would to something dangerous. What was he like? He had bandy legs, glasses that made him look older, hazelnut eyes, and an earthy odor reminiscent of Marilena's watered garden.

At boarding school Silvia had dreamed about that boy not once but many times, and even in her dreams he remained somewhat blurry, but she could see his gestures and hear his voice. They'd made contact in only one of them: he had scratched a dry scab off her knee. A patch of pink skin had emerged just where she now had a hole in her tights.

Silvia thought about her appearance for a few moments, something she hadn't done for days—in fact something she never did. She inspected her worn-out shoes, her laddered tights, the oily sheen she could feel on her face, her dirt-rimmed nails and flabby stomach. She was nothing like Giovanna, more an overgrown girl in long johns, puffy, wilted, and wrinkled. Her life wasn't over, but it was passing her by. And all the while it was going down the drain.

47

ON THURSDAY during the lunch break, Giulia and her friend Angela marched up to the step Martino was sitting on to eat but they didn't say anything to him. He pretended to be busy with his veal mayonnaise sandwich. The girls pulled little sugar pellets off their brioches, popping them into their mouths one by one.

"You're eating your napkin."

"Huh?"

"Your napkin. You're eating it," Angela informed him bluntly.

Martino felt as if he hated her. It was true: the bread and paper had cemented into one and were edged with his toothmarks.

"Oh, this. Right, thanks."

He looked up but Angela wasn't there anymore, only Giulia, with a mixed expression of skepticism and surprise on her face as if her friend's disappearance hadn't been planned but had caught her off guard as well. She took a couple of steps toward Martino and with the tip of her shoe began tracing a line through the dirt in the playground.

Deep down, Martino knew that eating a napkin doesn't injure a man's dignity as much as getting pigeon poo on his head. The summer before, in Turin's Vanchiglia neighborhood, he'd stopped to watch a couple arguing beside the road. Just as the man raised his voice, a squirt of gray hit him right on the forehead. He removed his dirty glasses immediately and did his best with a handkerchief, but his girlfriend burst out laughing and couldn't stop. She'd try to stifle it only to go on spluttering intermittently.

Across the road Martino, too, had been amused, all the more so since the sting had never gone out of that old incident of the dog poo thrown on his jacket and, well, misery loves company. But after a while, the woman's laughing seemed excessive even to him. The man's eyes blazed like those of a boss confronting an insubordinate underling, while his companion doubled over, half blinded by tears, drying them from time to time with the inside of her wrist. He raised his hand and slapped her. The laughter stopped instantly, and the girl furiously tore a ring off her finger and threw it on the pavement, where it disappeared down a drain. At that point, to Martino's great surprise, the couple's alarmed expression had simultaneously turned to one of complicity: they'd searched the drain on hands and knees for ages. That's what pigeon shit can do to you.

"I wonder why Greppi is staring at you," Giulia began.

Martino suddenly turned and for an instant his eyes met those of the teacher, who was standing against the wall smoking. His thick black beard hid his lips whenever he took a drag.

"Did you say he's looking at me?"

"Before, too, while you were playing football."

"Maybe he doesn't like us making the ball with sticky tape and loo roll."

"Why should that matter? Out of all of us, he was looking at you."

"So what."

"He doesn't even know you." Giulia whispered as if she held a grudge, and Martino made the connection.

"Let's hope he leaves soon—that Canepa comes back soon so he'll go." He was floundering, but apparently she didn't notice.

"If she comes back . . ." Giulia murmured.

"I think she will."

"Thanks," she replied, as if he'd said something polite but groundless, a cross between a wish and a condolence. "I don't know if you know," she added, "that she's my dad's cousin and she's almost always lived with us."

Anselmo, Martino noted—the cousin Silvia had invoked in her trance in the hut—was Giulia's father.

"I knew she was part of your family."

Giulia sat down beside him. Her blue-and-gray plaid skirt peeked out from under her smock and she smoothed it with the palms of her hands; she also tidied her shoulder-length hair, which swung forward.

Martino was a bundle of nerves. He was trying to dislodge a piece of chewed-up sandwich stuck to the roof of his mouth without her noticing, irritated with his mother for making him that sticky snack. *Don't do anything stupid,* he said to himself.

He started up again. "I think she's still around here somewhere."

"My father has looked everywhere. Even in the churches. Someone told us she might be hiding in a church." Giulia looked at him hesitantly, as if considering whether to add something.

"Did she often go to church?"

"Not that much."

"So nothing's really come up."

"Nothing. My parents have gone all the way to Santhià, Salussola, as far as Turin. Someone was sure they'd seen her in Borgo Dora. Or at the station, they think they saw her near the platforms but it's not true. They're mistaking her for someone else. Not so much purposely, I think, as from a desire to do good."

Martino let himself be drawn in by that version of the story.

"Does she know anyone in Turin, someone who could help her?"

"Yes, we also have relatives there."

"And couldn't she be hiding with them?"

"But they'd tell us!"

"Maybe she needs time to pull herself together."

"And you think she wouldn't let us know? That she'd leave us here looking for her like . . . like idiots?"

"Yes—I mean no. You're right," Martino gave in. At that moment he was certain: he'd messed it all up. He should never have kept the teacher's secret. What a colossal mistake he'd made. But it was too late. If he admitted his mistakes it would be a disaster. Giulia would never forgive him. He got the hiccups, having swallowed the last bites of his sandwich too quickly, and had to hold his breath to stop them while she waited quietly.

"You came for a really great year," she commented sarcastically.

"What do you mean?"

"It's not always like this."

A bit late, Martino finally smiled at her. "I believe it."

"I know the village you live in."

"Ah."

"My father's from there. Silvia too."

"No way!"

"Does that bother you?"

"No."

"Well compared with Turin it must be boring."

"Yeah, well. It's different." He decided he absolutely wouldn't mention the woods and cleared his throat.

"Your mother is really pretty," Giulia was saying. "I remember her; she came at the beginning of the year."

"Yours too," he replied impulsively.

"Have you ever seen her?"

He blushed. "I think so. Maybe I got mixed up."

"On Saturday we're going to your village. Maybe we'll see each other." Giulia moved on to other things, her embarrassment a current pulling her along, while Martino sat there dazed, a rabbit in the headlights.

"I'll be there," he replied. He promised himself on the spot that he'd refuse to go on any walk and stand lookout on the main road—for the whole day if he had to.

"Do you know the chapel in the woods?"

"You mean the sort of ugly one?" he dared.

"Horrible! I want to repaint it myself in a few years; I'm practicing. I even have a book that tells how to do it: *Fresco Painting*. You have to be quick because basically the wet plaster absorbs the color and then when it dries it sets. When I'm older I want to be a painter, or maybe restore old masterpieces."

She said it just like that, "old masterpieces," and she was thinking about the installments of *Masters of Color* and volumes on the finds at Herculaneum and Pompeii that Silvia kept in her messy room. She'd spent entire afternoons bent over pictures and drawings, on statues both nude and clothed, with blank eyes. Sitting beside Silvia while she marked homework or set exercises, Giulia copied the most stunning pieces into her notebook: Odilon Redon's spider and cyclops, Roman masks with jug ears and grotesque noses like gnocchi made of wax, the sculpture of a boy holding a dolphin, lion-paw table legs topped with female busts.

As he listened, Martino tried to think of something worthy of telling her. He wanted to have a project as grandiose and original as hers. He quickly rejected the pirate and adventurer. Could he say that he wanted to become a sailor? A musician? He'd often thought of asking his parents for an instrument to help him control his need to move around, beat things and punch them. A drum kit, he told himself, and it seemed like a bright idea that Giulia had whispered to him.

"Let's go back in. It's time." She went ahead of him and the bell rang loudly, vibrating through the soles of their feet.

48

Martino was turning that conversation over in his head on the way home from school. It seemed like a long and meaningful one. He accepted the bus's jolts as affectionate pats. Traffic lights blazed against the gray sky and pylons seemed to him miracles of latticed beauty festooned with high-tension cables.

He jumped out in front of the church and recognized Sandra, the lady with the pointy bosom, maneuvering to get an unsteady figure down on the bench. She planted herself in front of the elderly lady, legs akimbo, keeping her own arms loose and leaning back in order to set her down as slowly and gradually as possible, and then rearranged her cardigan, which had climbed up her back, and went to the chemist's.

The elderly lady noticed right away that Martino was looking at her. "Do I know you? Come a bit closer. Come here."

Of course she must be Sandra's mother, the one who'd thrown herself out of the window. The metal stick her daughter had placed beside her slipped to her feet and Martino reluctantly bent over to pick it up while she grumbled, "She's really not good at anything, that one." The woman held the stick, her hand speckled with age spots, and put it next to her as if it were a sword. Her sparse white hair had been backcombed and gathered in a tiny bun, revealing her pink skull through her parting.

"Whose son are you?" she asked.

"I'm not from this village."

"From where then?"

"Turin."

"So what are you doing here?"

"I've come for my health."

"You! You seem fit as a fiddle."

Martino was half listening to her and half imagining her unstrung and in the act of clambering over the windowsill. Once again he was struck by the similarity with Giovanna's story and he thought that, of the two, it would have been better if the girl had survived.

"Okay, I don't get out much, but completely senile I am not," said the elderly lady. "I knew yours wasn't a face I recognized."

She had a leather handbag in her lap with a snap clasp and she started working it with twisted fingers until she got it open.

"And yet you are definitely flesh and bone."

She felt around in her bag and huffed. Her gold chain with a medallion of the Madonna swung back and forth.

"Beastly arthritis. You don't know how many dollars."

"Dollars?" Martino leaned toward the handbag, expecting to see a handful of banknotes.

"I meant how dolorous it is."

"Oh."

"What's my daughter doing in there? It must be half an hour since she went in." The woman was growing impatient.

"Well, no, it can only be five minutes."

The elderly lady brandished the watch on her scrawny wrist. "Half an hour, I'm telling you." She went back to rummaging in her bag and soon took out a Cri-Cri, a chocolate hazelnut praline wrapped in shiny paper. "Wait, I have some more."

Martino had a weakness for Cri-Cri. Usually he bit them in half with his teeth to relish the hazelnut center followed by the chocolate, then the hundreds and thousands.

"So are you going to eat it or not?"

A man with a bushy mustache stopped to say hello. Like many men his age, serious drinkers, his cheeks were hatched with rosacea and the tip of his nose was a network of broken capillaries. "How are we getting along, Miranda?" he asked the old lady.

"How am I getting along? With a stick."

"I see you're in good company."

"From Turin."

"Fancy that."

"Well! It's not that big a deal."

Martino was itching to be on his way but was worried about bumping into the Leader and his two sidekicks. He wanted to shelter at home, bask in the details of Giulia's proximity—the golden down on her knees, for example, though her hair was chestnut—and go up to the woods later taking a roundabout route to avoid any unfortunate encounters—and talk to Silvia about Giulia, tell her how much Giulia felt her absence. One scene was etched in his mind: him coming down from the woods on Saturday, supporting the teacher and taking her to Giulia.

The old lady noticed that he wasn't really there with them. She said, "I think I've tormented you enough," and, moving her entire face, she managed to give him a wink.

"Thank you for the chocolates."

"Go, go on. Don't stand there thanking me."

To avoid the café, Martino walked along the vineyard where the last harvest of the year was taking place. The grape pickers laid clusters of grapes in plastic buckets as they sang:

On the hat, on the hat we wear
There's a long black, long black feather
It serves, it serves as our flag
Up the mountains, to the mountains we go
To wage war.
Tralala!

As he turned toward the church, Martino saw that Sandra had come out of the chemist's. She stood behind the bench with a hand on her mother's shoulder. Her mother wound her own fingers through Sandra's and, thus interlaced, they continued chatting with the man.

49

LEA FOUND A LETTER in the letter box addressed to her but bearing no return address. Inside was a card with a clipping pasted on it: a woman with red hair drawn by Modigliani. She was wearing a plain black dress with a soft-gray collar. Her eyes had no pupils, or maybe they were all pupil, because they were entirely filled with black. The curved lines echoed one another: nose, face, neck, wrist, knee. It seemed like she had no bust, a doughnut high under her armpits. Lea really did look like her, as if the painting were a calmer, tamed version of herself.

She couldn't find any writing, much less a signature, but she was sure the teacher had sent it. Not Stefano or Gianni, not a colleague. As for her, she'd dreamed about him in one of those classic dreams, such as the one where you find a tap that's gone dry when you're thirsty while asleep: they met in a harshly lit, crowded conference room and tried unsuccessfully to find someplace to be alone.

Lea tucked the clipping between her underclothes in a drawer and lay down on the bedspread. The day before, Gianni had asked her why she was so convinced that she was a bad person, and she replied that she just wanted to be different since people usually make themselves out to be virtuous and go around saying that they're good and kind, thinking they're always right.

"I'm not that gullible," was his reply.

The phone rang and Lea got up, tense and trembling at the thought of the teacher. It was Stefano: his knee was swollen again because of a torn meniscus and he couldn't drive. His mother had brought over platters of food from the deli, claiming to have cooked them herself ("Vols au vent and tongue in salsa verde? As if!"), but Stefano hoped that Lea and Martino would take the train the next day and stay with him until Sunday.

"Sure," said Lea. "Of course we'll come."

"But wait a sec, did you get it?" he asked.

"Get what?"

"Nothing. Nothing. I can tell it hasn't arrived. What a jerk. I've ruined it now."

"Would you tell me what you're talking about?" she barked. "Come on, Stefano!"

"I sent you something silly."

"A letter?"

"It was supposed to be a surprise."

"Well you've said too much now, so you might as well." She persisted so doggedly that she ended up offending him.

"A chemise. I put it in an envelope. Tell me if you like it."

Lea offered an awkward apology, ashamed of herself and thinking all the while that the sender of the postcard really must be the teacher. A tingle went down her spine.

Once the phone call was over, she began boiling quince for jelly and mocking herself for feeling that a stranger could step right into her marriage and carry her away. She took the Modigliani card from the drawer and went to throw it in the dustbin. But she changed her mind, went back to her room, and put it in the ugly chest where she kept her woolens.

50

As soon as he got home Martino knew his mother was in a bad mood. She kept her head down and shook her hands as if to get rid of who knows what. All her gestures—rinsing a glass, putting lunch on to warm, slicing the bread—were speedy yet overemphatic.

"Your room is a pigsty. Clean it up after lunch," she ordered.

She wanted to know why he wasn't hungry, but he didn't feel like telling her about the Cri-Cri Sandra's mother had given him. She seemed like a witch but she wasn't all that bad.

When Lea announced that they'd be taking the train to Turin the next day, he shot up like a spring. She was dumbfounded: it was the first time Martino had blamed her clearly and articulately for imposing her will on him, and he spoke like an adult who could harness his rage and ride it. He threw it all back at her, the fact that she'd torn him away from Turin, put him in a school in town without asking his opinion, shoved him around and laid down the law, always giving orders. But he was sick of it. He didn't want to go back to Turin now. It was out of the question. He had things to do: a friend was coming on Saturday, his friend from that shitty school, and Papa would get along just fine without them.

"But your father needs us," she retorted. "This is a tantrum, and I don't give in to tantrums."

"What do you mean a tantrum! It's a matter of life or death!" Martino shouted to her face. And then it came out: "You don't know it but the teacher's involved."

"What do you mean, the teacher?"

"Because—because . . . my friend is related to her. She's coming to look for her and I want to help."

"Are you kidding? That woman may have been dead for days. There'll be trouble if you go looking for her, do you understand? Don't you understand that you could find yourself—" Lea stopped and blinked, as if she'd suddenly realized something obvious. "Don't tell me you go to the woods because you're hoping to find the teacher? Tell me the truth."

"No, I go there to play Sandokan."

"You'll have to stay close to home. Look, you're not going out today."

Martino suddenly stopped mid-flow, choked with disappointment. He threw his schoolbag to the floor and ran to his room, slamming the door behind him.

The scent of damp plants hit the house in gusts. It was so strong in the woods that it tickled his nose and he could tell sharp pine needles from the caramelized putrescence of dead leaves. But the woods were inaccessible and so was the teacher, who was in danger of becoming very ill if he left. Thursday, Friday, Saturday, Sunday: four whole days. He absolutely had to go out, buy some food with his savings, and take it to the hut.

Martino threw open both shutters and decided to leap out and run for it. It wasn't that far down, and if Sandra's mother had survived a jump like this one, surely he would too. He leaned out to judge the width of the cement pavement that ran around the house; he'd have to leap over it in order to land on soft lawn. Just as he was mustering up courage by imagining a wild boar at his heels, his mother came into the room. She was coming to make peace, but at the sight of him leaning out with one knee on the windowsill her blood boiled again.

"What the hell are you doing?"

Martino put his foot back on the floor and, despite his good intentions, he felt on the verge of confessing: another Martino, barely any younger but still there inside, urged him to throw himself into Lea's arms, cry hard enough to scare her so she'd soften up and forgive him for the lies he'd told, for having kept the teacher hidden and snitched food for her, for letting everyone worry and search for her with dogs and volunteers, for allowing her relatives to go on wild goose hunts in the village, under bridges, all the way to Salussola and Turin. But in the last few weeks, something had changed. He also felt in his chest a heart both hard and elastic, a rubber ball that bounced crazily and without warning for the most disparate reasons: the thought of Piero and Agostino being so far away, his friendship with the teacher, Giulia, those three idiots wanking off in the woods.

They started arguing again. "You're coming to Turin," to which he replied, "Absolutely not!" In the end, both tired, they came to a compromise that suited neither of them: they'd leave early on Sunday and come back the same day on the last train.

51

LEA KNEW THE TEACHER lived near the school. "See how it all connects?" he said, and from the door of the café he'd pointed to his small balcony on the fourth floor where his bicycle was wedged diagonally, handlebars leaning over the blue-painted railing. He used it, he told her, to go for long rides in the afternoon, sometimes on the mountain's hairpin bends, occasionally toward the rice fields, now dry. With Stefano away in Turin and Martino absorbed by his new friend, she'd have Saturday free to spend checking her urge to go to town.

As a distraction she took out a hammer and screwdriver and threw herself into destroying a potter wasp's nest that had been built between an internal shutter and the wall at the end of August. Together she and Martino had observed the wasp's comings and goings but from a distance, since they weren't sure if it stung or might be dangerous, like a hornet.

Martino sat on a bench beside the front door—somewhere he never sat—homework on his knees, sulking. Patches of light briefly filtered through the clouds as if signaling to him, babbling in an unknown code.

Around the corner came Maria, the one they called Big Mouth, with her thumping step and a plastic bag knocking against her flowered dress. Her sharp eyes, small mouth, and nose were all set close together in the middle of a wide, square face framed by the fat beneath her chin. She wrung the necks of the village chickens and geese and was famed for her skills. As she approached, Martino peered at her hands and nails but they were clean. There were white feathers sticking out of her sack and she confirmed without his having to ask, "A young bird. They gave me one for my work. But you're from the city—as far as you're concerned chickens grow in shops, already plucked."

For the fun of it—and to disgust him—Maria improvised a lesson on how to dispatch poultry. Her bag, abandoned on the tarmac, relaxed and grew larger, shaping itself over the hen whose long, stiff flight feathers poked against the plastic.

"You hold the chicken by the feet with your bad hand—mine's my left—while you squeeze its neck and plant your thumb in the hollow behind its head. Then you have to give it a sharp yank with both arms." And she mimicked the gesture, a sudden and brutal movement that made Martino jump. "So the vertebra snaps and that's it, the chicken is gone. Never twist the neck: the beast can escape with its head dangling and it won't die. So: the worst is over. After that you snip its throat with some big scissors and hang it up to drain the blood."

"But how come they always call you?"

"Because the beasts don't suffer as much with me. You mustn't feel sorry for the animal or it'll have a bad death. Even fear makes it suffer, so you have to be decisive, understand? And quick, so it doesn't even notice."

Martino looked up at her with reverence as an angel of death. She was wearing perforated white leather clogs, a summer pinafore dress, and a woolen cable jumper.

"The hard work comes later. Plucking, or skinning a rabbit," she added, relishing the effect of every word before starting the march toward home again.

Martino's mother called him from inside. "Martino, come here! Come and see!" She'd scooped the broken wasp's nest into the dustpan and insisted on showing him something.

"That's enough dead animals for now!" he burst out.

"Why? What other dead animals have you seen?"

"Maria's hen—but I didn't really see it."

"Okay, never mind." Lea wanted to bend over and kiss his head, but Martino had already turned his back and moved away, and he didn't notice.

Later, when he'd finished his homework and felt a little better, Martino asked his mother, "What was it you wanted to show me?"

"Oh, it was nothing. Something actually kind of grim."

"What?"

"I think the larvae ate the wasp."

"That's revolting! Are you sure?"

"I thought I saw a piece of the wasp in there. The things mothers will do!"

It was ironic, but he wanted to check no matter what, as if to restore the honor of the offspring.

The nest was still in the metal dustpan, broken into large regular cylindrical cells surrounded by little pieces. He saw organic fragments, an abdomen, maybe, and lots of tiny, crushed feet which under the magnifying glass proved to be spiders' legs. Exultant, he ran to report: the wasp had not let herself be eaten after all but had caught prey for her babies and then gone off to do her own thing.

52

FOR THE FIRST TIME since she's come to the woods, Silvia feels short bursts of something like boredom. It has to do with her perception of time, which is focused, however vaguely, on Martino's visits. He doesn't come, though, and her habit of not controlling her thoughts or movements takes over.

A red-and-black ant runs over the back of her hand. She squashes it with her thumb and smells her fingertip: a bubble of sharp scent. She picks up a pebble and puts it in her mouth without thinking about it, like someone who doesn't notice their habit of biting their fingernails. Her tongue rasps over its flaky surface; cold metallic pins sting her. After a while she spits the pebble into her palm: it shines, almost completely covered with flecks of silvery mica. She picks up another, but it's only a clump of earth and it crumbles immediately. A third, the size of a cherry and speckled with black and lilac, satisfies her for a long time. The leaves and straw are acidic; their fibers, tough as horsehair, nauseate her. If anything, she prefers the flavor of the dirt marinating under her fingernails. She goes back to the pebbles, most of them irregular blots of dull gray. She sucks on them and recalls Giovanna's pretend sweets.

*

In the first year, Giovanna was the only one who didn't bring sweets to school. She wore a plain smock with threadbare elbows and her blond hair escaped her hair slide and fell over her face. She was repeating a year, but it seemed she'd learned nothing. Her body, however, had had time to grow and, compared with her classmates, she was tall and awkward, so she'd hunker down behind her desk as much as she could, bending her spine so that her vertebrae stuck out from under the black fabric of her smock.

To the others she was the girl from the valleys, daughter of a primitive race. She spoke pure dialect, with an accent different to the one Silvia had learned during her childhood in the hillside villages. It was above all harsher than the accent of the city, and it gave the impression that the sound got stuck at the back of the palate. It was the same accent that rang out over the cowbells on the road during the transhumance at the beginning and end of summer, above the plumes of smoke from coal burners' chimneys in the high valleys: the vernacular of people who are isolated and marginal, who come from proverbial savagery and filth.

All the children in the class Italianized Piedmontese words and confused things. They continued to write *sagrinarsi*, to worry or grieve, *bogiare,* move, and *ramina*, or saucepan, for a long time. When they spoke, they mixed Italian with dialect in varying proportions. Not Giovanna. For her, Piedmontese was the only language and Italian a hostile foreign idiom because it put her in her place: at the bottom. There was no room for her mother tongue at school. It wasn't worthy of writing or reading.

During break, Giovanna kept to herself. Often she didn't even leave the classroom. Silvia had once surprised her going through the waste bin to collect the sweet wrappers thrown out by her classmates, which she hid in her pockets. She slipped into the playground and from the gravel she inconspicuously chose stones with the most regular shapes, wrapping the little rectangles of colored foil around them. She was pretending, more for herself than for others.

As it turned out, Giovanna was a sharp, accurate shot at marbles and thanks to this skill she integrated into the class—thanks to the marbles and a couple of slaps she gave boys who were poor losers. Silvia neglected to mark those down against her conduct.

At the end of the first year, the teacher decided that Giovanna needed something to read to match the world of dialect she was going back to, so she lent her Angelo Brofferio's *Canzoni piemontese*, an 1881 edition with the title stamped in gold lettering on the spine. It had belonged to her grandfather, who loved to recite the songs to his friends, especially "Humanity" and "Cod or Cavour and Cholera" or the one that was called "The Glory of Paradise." Her grandmother would start crossing herself at the first rhyme and escape to another room, but her grandfather put a hand on little Silvia's arm so she would stay and listen:

Se i poum d'or son per parei
Che noiousa landa!
Da Bergnif a stan aut mei;
Viva la ca granda!

Mei là giù con i diaulot
*Che si dsour con i bigot.**

Giovanna liked it so much, that enlightened, anticlerical book, that she never returned it. The teacher had taken out a library card for every student, but she'd never entrusted one of her own hardcover books with golden lettering to anyone. At home, Giovanna's father peered at the verses.

"Did your teacher really give you that? Are you sure?"

Giovanna was proud of it. She leafed through the pages feeling as though there were a balloon inflated in her chest helping her to stand up straight. Now and again, to make herself sound important she'd write in her essays: "As Brofferio, the illustrious poet, says . . ."

* If golden apples taste like this / The boredom must be endless! / The Devil's apples taste of bliss / Long live the Big House! / It's better down there with devils / Than up on high with bigots.

53

ON THURSDAY EVENING, Luisa had to go up to her neighbor's to give her an injection and Giulia wanted to go with her.

"We'll have to ask if she minds showing her bum cheeks."

Palma, their neighbor, had no objections. She was a large woman in her seventies with a frail and avoidant husband who opened the door to them and went back to watching *Double Your Money*. Her hair was very short and she had a pretty face, shiny and smooth with its wrinkles ironed out by fat, violet lips, and an enormous bum glowing in the light of the table lamp.

She wanted to know how the search was going, how Anselmo was, how they were doing. But she also felt compelled to complain about her husband and before long she said, "As soon as I can I'm going to get a divorce."

"You don't mess around, Palmina."

"You'll see. You'll see, it'll go through." She was referring to the law that would make divorce legal, one that parliament had been quashing for the last five years.

Giulia, meanwhile, held out the things her mother needed: a cotton-wool ball soaked in disinfectant, the metal tray with syringe and needles, a phial of Lamuran with a rubber cap for the needle. Luisa filled the syringe, replaced the needle to ensure that it was sharp, and then snapped the syringe with the nail of her index finger and squirted out a few drops of medicine. She disinfected Palmina's skin and stuck the needle in without wasting time. She withdrew the plunger to aspirate the needle and was able to inject. Giulia was memorizing the various steps.

"Yes, but even if they approve it . . . your husband has to be crazy or in prison or that's it." Luisa extracted the syringe. "Done."

"I didn't even notice. You really have golden hands," said Palma, and she went right back to her argument. "Leaving the marital home," she pronounced.

"But he's right there in the living room!"

"And who'll take him away? I'm going to go. I'll go to my children in Desenzano. I already have three grandchildren and I never see them because of him."

"Will they take you in?"

"Laura's already said yes. 'Mamma, come whenever you want to. I'll fix up the dining room for you.'"

"Well, go then."

"You bet I will, and after five years I'll ask for a divorce."

"Of course, of course. Then you'll see."

"I'll ask him. Just for the satisfaction. I don't want to end up buried beside him, our photos one above the other with the inscription: In Greggio. I want to die as Palma Ferraro, full stop. You'll see—without me he'll bet even his underwear, never mind his pension. And to think that he has a good one."

As Palma hoisted herself to her feet and adjusted her clothes, Luisa turned a wry smile on Giulia to play down the situation.

When they got back downstairs Giulia asked her mother to fill her in. She didn't understand what sort of game Palma's husband, Primino, played so avidly or what was wrong. Luisa explained that he had a weakness for playing cards and lost money at them, which was why his wife was angry with him. She told her, but only because everyone knew and it wasn't a secret. She filled the bathtub. A chill from tiredness and worry had risen from her feet, her fingers were icy-cold, and her head was heavy on her neck.

The usual bath day was Sunday, and besides, it was late already: Anselmo had gone to bed with his crossword. Gemma and Corrado were sure to be asleep by now. They both got undressed as steam rose and clung to the mirror. Luisa examined some red bumps that had grown on her breast and under her armpits. "Angiomas," she explained. "Harmless angiomas. I have polka-dot skin."

She had only one breast. The other had been removed three years earlier because of a tumor and all that was left of it was a curved line on her flat chest; she filled her bra with a specially made silicone pad. Giulia felt odd when she thought about the breast that had nursed her having been cut off and thrown away. Luisa said she'd gone back to being half child, and every now and then Gemma brought up Saint Agatha, who carried her severed breasts on a platter.

While they were immersed in the bathtub Anselmo came to the door and grumbled, "You're both crazy. Didn't you see what time it is?"

"Shut the door; you're letting the heat out," Luisa replied.

She put bathing caps over her hair and Giulia's to keep it dry. They used a lot of soap. Luisa washed Giulia's toes one by one and exfoliated her heels with a pumice stone. Every so often she let out a long sigh of pleasure. "This was just what I needed. I really needed this."

Giulia compared her mother's one nipple, which was grainy and distinct from its pale areola, with her own flat ones and their tiny fleshy nut at the center.

"When you were a girl did you heat water over the fire in saucepans?"

"Yes, that's what we did. And at least three people used the same water. We used to draw lots to decide who would get into the water first."

"Will you get a divorce from Papa too?"

Luisa's eyes widened and Giulia clasped her own shoulders. "No, I don't really think so."

"Why not?"

"Because I still love him."

"Grandma says they don't allow divorced people in church."

"That may well be."

"So then you can't divorce."

"Right. But luckily I don't want to, right?"

"Palmina won't go into church anymore?"

"Many years go by before a divorce becomes final. In the meantime you can go in and even take Communion."

"After that?"

"I don't think she's bothered about it."

"But at her funeral later, how will they say Mass for her?"

"I don't know. You'll see: they won't deny her a church funeral. Are you worrying about that?"

Giulia thought about it while she gathered foam in her hands and stuck it to her chin, a sparkling beard. "No."

"Good. Then turn around and I'll wash your back."

It made Giulia a little ticklish. Luisa got out first and held Giulia's bathrobe open, tied it around her waist.

Later in bed she found Anselmo lying on his side with his back to her, barricaded in reproach. And sure enough, as soon as she lay down he started reeling off the waste of water, the time, school next day, lost sleep, bad habits. Luisa opened her little box of earplugs, shoved them in, and closed her eyes while he went on talking with his back to her. But from the tension of the sheets and the rocking of the mattress she could tell that her husband was still grumbling even in the silence.

When Anselmo finally fell asleep, Luisa leaned over him in the dark. Soft chest hairs stuck through his ribbed vest; she loved to caress them and Corrado would pull them out to initiate play-fighting. His long body, submerged in sleep, gave off warmth. Anselmo was three years younger than she was and this had always reassured her: during the war he was only a boy and he hadn't had time to do anything bad.

Luisa got up and went to the kitchen, where she found some leftover roast potatoes in the fridge and began eating them, sitting there in the dark. Silvia's disappearance, Palmina and her plans to run off, her own youth, marriage and work in the factory, illnesses, hospital stays and recovery, childbirth: that chorus of seemingly dissonant events corresponded to a secret harmony she was trying hard to name, as when you can hear a song in your head but you can't sing it out loud. Some kind of glue was holding the pieces of her life together, an assumption, the same one that kept her from throwing plates at Anselmo when he badgered her. She tried to formulate it clearly to herself while chewing on cold potatoes and watching the jagged black mountains turn gray and white as the moon scythed through clouds, illuminating the snowfall on their peaks.

What's keeping you upright? she wondered. It was her sense of duty. She'd been taught—by whom? everyone and everything: example, religion, people she loved—that you had to do things right, do the right thing, keep on going. *How are things? Oh, we're trundling along* was the automatic reply, and yet it was perfectly sincere. Trundling along was a moral precept because life is a cart to pull, a work to bring to completion. When you're tired, you persevere. When you're suffering, you endure. When you want to leave, you stay. Industry as an antidote to unhappiness. Not that Luisa hadn't been happy; she'd often been so. Her joys naturally came from persevering, enduring, and staying. After the death of her first love, she had married. After the death of her first baby, Giulia and Corrado had been born. She'd had a life of second chances. Of resurrections, as Sister Annangela had once told her.

She recalled Silvia's face when she came to visit Luisa in the hospital after she first gave birth, that inexpressive face that had allowed her to rest under its gaze. Silvia had sat down in the visitor's chair, which she'd placed at a three-quarter-degree angle facing the window, and she stayed there for a long time, ankles attached to legs of steel. Silent, as if at a wake—for all practical purposes, it was one. Silvia was the only person who hadn't tried to console her, nor did she try to guess, by watching her, whether she would ever get over the loss of her child.

54

Luisa had been convinced that she would be able to hold back her screams during labor, but she had yelled as her body behaved in a way that was at odds with what she knew about it. A band of muscles that had always been quiet in the past now squeezed to make space for the baby's head, drawing it out of her uterus where it had been protected for months.

She smelled something bittersweet, like prawns boiling in their shells, and all she could feel was that her legs were pointing in different directions and remained rigid as sticks whenever they were moved or bent. Her waters gushed out rhythmically, and near the end they were tinged first with pink, then with red. At that point something hard forced her pelvis open. It was accompanied by a burning sensation, as if from an open wound. Her muscles pushed of their own volition and tried to release themselves in the pushing, and she couldn't do a thing about it.

She stopped yelling only because they ordered her to stop. They told her she had to focus her energies. She gritted her teeth and groaned. Toward the end she vomited up the water she'd drunk. The obstetrician kept passing a finger over her labia, tight as a drum, saying that she could see the baby's hair, "black as a raven's wing." Another push, and a brief flash of pain accompanied the first actual delivery in sixteen hours: the head emerged. Luisa then allowed herself to remember the home births of her relatives: no equipment, not enough disinfectant, kerosene lamps lit all night, tin stirrups, and mountains of sheets to wash by hand the next day.

She thought she'd done it. The rest of the baby slid out with a shudder like a large fish and she didn't even notice the placenta: they'd shown it to her while she was thinking that the butcher's block was the thing she found most like birth, with its wet, pink flesh, rumps and hindquarters, the rubbery bloom of small organs. She flopped back on her pillows and waited for them to restore her baby to her, clean and swaddled. Only the baby wasn't breathing: perhaps the heart, a problem with its metabolism, or undeveloped lungs.

Anselmo held her close and cried. She found it hard to take in the fact that she now had to halt that convoy of love, germ cells, effort, imagination, vomit, preparations, and ligaments loosened to make room for a little person who had really existed and had had eyebrows, nails, the name they'd chosen for him, and the little blue bottom that she'd spied while he was still alive.

For a long time Luisa had continued to feel the baby hiccup-ing: regular taps around her navel. She wasn't brave enough to try again, but neither did she have the courage to escape. Day and night, she fantasized about becoming a nun. At the time, she envied Silvia inside her shell—alone, free, perhaps a little sad but at least not panic-stricken, not pregnant. Silvia thought the same thing—*Why should I bother? Why should she bother?*—and they told each other so years later.

"And yet," Silvia added, "look what beautiful children you have."

"Yes, it turned out well for me in the end."

"I wouldn't have made it."

Luisa had wanted to be sedated for Giulia's birth so they could pull her out without Luisa's being aware of it, and instead the same thing happened all over again. But the baby had cried instantly with the irritated bleating of a vexed creature. She was fat and beautiful and plastered with a newborn's waxy white film, her cheeks rounded as bagpipes. She had grown up and was about to become a young girl. Silvia was gone—dead or alive, she'd decided to leave them. Luisa sat in the kitchen at night, trying to see herself through her daughter's eyes and wondering what she was teaching her.

55

THE NEXT AFTERNOON, a Friday, Giulia got drunk at home with her friend Angela. They had come back from school hoping to hurry through their homework so that in each other's locked diaries they could copy out and illustrate phrases popular with girls in their class: *Best friends are the sisters you choose for yourself (Eustache Deschamps), Forget me not, the little river flower whispers / Forget me not, I too whisper! (Anonymous)*

They both had bad colds, blocked noses and painful sinuses, so before getting down to work they decided to make themselves two cups of hot milk with a drop of grappa, the way the grown-ups usually made it for them. The only thing was, they didn't know how to measure the grappa. It should have been a droplet, but in their hands it became a shot glass. Within ten minutes they were doubled over their notebooks laughing, oblivious to ink smears and instead exhilarated by their increasingly deformed, uneven writing.

They threw themselves on the sofa and Angela decided to pretend to be Martino. Giulia had to give her a proper kiss on the lips, she insisted, and Giulia scoffed and backed away, saliva dribbling from her mouth. The two of them were thin and straight as a rail, so that the bones of their elbows and knees, sternums and pelvises were aligned. When she got home with Corrado, Gemma found them in that state and Corrado enthusiastically threw himself into the mix.

Gemma sniffed the empty cups and wrinkled her nose. The girls' cheeks were red, ears boiling, and they were wriggling to get away from the little boy's kicking. Their grandmother came to help them. She extricated Corrado, managed to get his shoes on him, and ordered Giulia and Angela to stand up. They swayed and giggled, explaining in comical drawls that they'd only drunk a little fortified milk as usual. Giulia asked Angela if she saw the pattern on the carpet wriggling like worms. Angela leaned over to examine it, rapt. Seconds later she said yes, she saw it, too, and was so exultant she could hardly refrain from kicking her legs in the air.

Gemma didn't try to hide the fact that she found it all amusing. She pushed them into the bathroom and washed hands, necks, and faces while the girls cackled, gurgled, and held to the edge of the sink in an effort to stay upright. Since their undershirts were soaking wet by then, she dressed them in some of Giulia's dry clothes. She made them eat bread and drink a great deal of water and then phoned for Angela's father to come and get her.

It was the first time since Silvia's disappearance that something approaching good humor had welled up in Gemma's chest. She wished she could do Giulia's homework for her, but she had completed the third year only and still read by mouthing the words; she did her math in a mixed and unorthodox way, by breaking things down and guessing. She got Corrado busy sticking cards and toothpicks onto a corkboard and helped Giulia by scratching her back, shooing away the flies that persisted in settling on her drooping head.

56

All that time, Martino was in the hut in the middle of the woods.

For the entire morning at school he had brooded over things to say to Giulia but hadn't managed to utter even one of them. It was astonishing how awkward her presence made him, and yet this awareness wasn't enough for him to control himself. His hands, for example: if he suspected that she was looking at him, his hands turned into a couple of mechanical shovels wholly unsuited for fine work such as tying his shoelaces or taking a sharpener out of his pencil case. His brain made desperate attempts at the control panel to maneuver those shovels, but the knot on his shoes turned out loose and cockeyed, the sharpener fell to the floor, and his foot—also clumsy—kicked it away by mistake.

Besides, there was his secret, which stood in his way. Sometimes he forgot about it for a while, at times it made him fractious, but most of the time he felt like he could keep it forever. That wasn't true, because the teacher was dependent on him and it was impossible to sustain a burden like that for long.

Lea had let him go out after he solemnly promised not to venture far from home—and he'd scaled the hill without losing a moment. Despite having food, water, and blankets the teacher looked increasingly unhealthy: the skin on her face was sagging under her cheekbones and purple rings haloed her eyes. Talking to her, however, had become easy, much easier than talking to Giulia.

"What did you do today?" she asked him, and he didn't refrain from mentioning Giulia and confessing that they had become friends, sort of.

Silvia seemed not to react. Her expression was gentle, faintly dopey.

"Why don't you go back?" Martino went right in.

"I'm afraid."

"Afraid of what?"

"Of being blamed."

"But nobody thinks that!"

"I feel it myself. In my conscience."

Martino fell silent. He was pondering things.

"As if someone were keeping an eye on you from the inside," she added to explain what a conscience was.

"A teacher."

Silvia looked away from the mud caked on her shoes and dirty skirt.

"Yes, a teacher," she said.

57

At dusk the air was clear and cold. A frosting of stars lit up the heavens and a breeze blew dry leaves into the hut along with the scent of cyclamen. Once she was alone, Silvia spoke again. Actually, there were certain things she only thought.

Her father beat her. And Anselmo, they beat him, too, when he was a child. They beat us at boarding school. So what was different about it? It was Giovanna.

She felt something wet on her face and the idea of crying in relief disgusted her. She wiped herself dry and then studied the objects Martino had brought her: canteen, blankets, an issue of *The History of the West*, bread she hadn't yet eaten, chocolate. She opened the comic book and tried to read some of the stories about bison and American Indians: the Dakota, the Crow, the Nez Perce. The block letters, all at close range and squeezed together, gave her a headache and she didn't understand the appeal of galloping or the volleys of hot lead that swept the Indians away from the fort's ramparts. It was a different matter, though: these were Martino's things and she pondered them carefully, as if she were choosing fish at the market, and taking care not to ruin them.

Martino risked being yelled at, grounded, and, as far as she knew, even beaten. If anyone else found her they would find all the provisions, too—she had never been concerned about that. *What an idiot you are, Silvia.*

Since she'd never dreamed that Giovanna might jump into the river, she had a moment's worry that Martino might do the same if he were discovered. She didn't believe it, because even in her isolation, the state she was in, she considered such a thing impossible, *another thing* like that. But she felt quite upset about it all the same, and it was the first feeling she'd had—sharp, alive, and unconnected to Giovanna—since she'd read the news in the newspaper one morning a few days earlier.

How many, she had no idea. She didn't know how long she'd been taking advantage of the boy so she tried to calculate using food: *What has he given me to eat? Bread, butter and sugar, salami, more bread, maybe some cheese at one point. We talked about dogs and what did he bring that day? Cake? No: apples.* She applied herself for some time but she couldn't work it out.

58

Lea took a long time in the shower, smoothing her thighs with the loofah mitt. She shaved her legs and armpits, passing the blade over skin slippery with bath foam, fixed her hair with the curling iron, put on blue eye shadow and mascara. Finally, all spruced up, she started cleaning the house.

Martino was a bundle of nerves. He vanished as soon as he finished his breakfast. All she'd managed to get out of him was the name of his eagerly awaited classmate: Giulia.

Gianni came by to leave the keys to his car, but Lea still didn't know if she would use it. She was washing vegetables and she dried her hands on her skirt as though getting it wet didn't bother her. She thought she could detect the sour odor of sweat under her perfume and was sure that Gianni had noticed her hair, her white blouse belted at the waist, and the way she was risking getting dirty by doing the housework in that outfit.

"Shall I put some artichokes aside for you?" she asked.

"Thanks. Martino?"

"He's outside waiting for his friend Giulia. His Pearl of Labuan, I'm afraid."

Gianni laughed and the scars on his cheeks wrinkled. A lock

of hair, stiff with brilliantine, had escaped the discipline of his comb and stood up on his head like an antenna. "But that's Anselmo Rosso's daughter. I'm waiting for them too. They're late. Should have been here two hours ago. We're beating the shores of the Quargnasca today."

"How can it be that we know nothing yet? Ten days must have passed by now."

"Look, I don't know. At least her body must be somewhere around here."

She held out a bag of cleaned artichokes.

"Did you know that the English say *artichoke* like we do? Exactly the same way."

"Articioc?"

"Artichoke: a-r-t-i-c-h-o-k-e."

"What do you know!"

"I think it's from the Arabic. Ciao, Lea. I don't need the car. Keep it till tomorrow."

"Well, you know we're taking the train to Turin tomorrow."

"Exactly. Leave it in the station car park so when you get back you'll find it waiting for you."

Afterward, Lea thought for a while that she would just stay put. She made something to eat and walked a little way down the road looking for Martino. When he saw her he hurried over. "Are you going to Biella?"

"Why?"

"You look elegant."

"Well, yes," she replied, "but I'll be back soon. There's something ready for you to eat at home. Still no Giulia?"

She got a dirty look.

"I'm asking because Gianni is expecting them too. When they get here, you two children can go to the house. Show her your room."

Distracted, Martino nodded and Lea turned back. He was short of breath and he felt like a fraud.

She rolled down the car windows to let in the cold and get rid of the smell of cigarettes and vetiver. She hooted the horn at Martino, standing by the edge of the road, and as she drove off she felt calm again. She passed women on their way to do the shopping and a boy with curly hair and trousers that were too short at his ankles. A chattering of starlings expanded and contracted in the sky like an accordion, a cloud of soot with a life of its own.

When she got to town, she parked near the school but not in the teacher's road, checking her face and hair in the rearview mirror once more before getting out. As she turned the corner she saw the bicycle in its place on the balcony with the blue-painted railing.

59

A PENSIONER OUT MUSHROOMING found her handbag at around six in the morning buried under a layer of chestnuts on the left bank of the Cervo. In it there were soaked notebooks, a pencil case, a wallet containing all her ID, keys, and throat lozenges. No newspaper—who knows where that ended up, blown away by the wind, disintegrated in the rain. Relative to the teacher's house, it was more or less on the way to the village.

Anselmo rushed to the spot together with the fire brigade, but there were no further traces of her. Days must have passed, and one couldn't be sure if the teacher had kept going that way or in another direction—to take the train, perhaps. Not even the dogs, put to work, could smell anything. Nevertheless, they expanded the search and spent the entire morning on it, after which Anselmo decided that it was worth trying in Bioglio as planned. So they only arrived—he, Gemma, Giulia, and Corrado—at lunchtime. They parked in a relative's courtyard and an exhausted Anselmo, heels blistered, hurried out to meet the team.

A few meters below the road two boys were fighting on the shady bank of the river. Anselmo called out to them but it was no good. One of them was smaller, a cockerel's thin neck sticking out of his jacket as it was being tugged; the other, strong and curly-headed, had him on the ground and was kneeing him in the stomach. Anselmo got to them in four leaps, put his large hands on the older boy, and shoved him over.

The Leader was ranting, "Hey, hey!" but when he recognized Anselmo he shut up. He knew the man, and more than that, the man knew his mother and father. He was helping Turin, coughing and gasping, to sit down. When all was said and done it didn't seem like anything that bad had happened to him apart from a punch that had smashed his lips against his teeth. Turin stared up at him, eyes glittering with hate, fists clenched, mouth swollen and flecked with blood. The Leader thought he was about to cry, but he took his inhaler from his pocket and greedily breathed in a stream of his medication. So it was true that the little pip-squeak was handicapped, the Leader noted.

Anselmo pulled the boy to his feet, put a hand on his shoulder, and started interrogating them. The two rivals retorted, heads down, voices low, replies blunt and in their view dignified.

"You really are a big coward, Walter. I'm eager to see what your father thinks about this. You can be sure I'll call him," Anselmo threatened. He then turned to Martino. "You go on home. Tell your mother to put some ice on you."

"My mother's gone out."

"Oh, damn! You two are wasting a lot of my time. I'll take you to my wife. Buzz off, Walter," he ordered, and he left dragging Martino behind him, not stopping until he was knocking at a door. After a few seconds he knocked again. A woman hurried to open it. Martino had seen her around, with her sharp face and glasses as round as the lights on a locomotive.

Anselmo pushed him in. "He's been beaten up. He needs ice and probably something sweet to drink. He's also short of breath. Will you see to him?"

"You're Lea's son, from Turin, right? My goodness." The woman lifted his chin and studied the bruise on his lip from behind her enormous lenses. Martino thought she was the big man's wife but then she said, "Look, Luisa. Look what Anselmo's brought us," and led him into the kitchen. There, seated at the table, was Giulia, eyes bulging, mouth open as in a comic strip. Meanwhile Martino connected the dots: the big man, Anselmo, was Giulia's father, the formidable lady with the brown hair must be her mother, and the baby dunking his bread in water and dribbling it all over the tablecloth might be her brother.

"Martino?" Giulia said, and from then on the explanations came together. Giulia and Martino were in the same class; the older lady—thin and as straight as an arrow—was Giulia's grandmother; someone had found Silvia's handbag; Anselmo and the others were getting ready to beat the shores of the River Quargnasca; Martino had been tussling with an older boy, Walter, who was identified as the son of a well-known person ("A bully from day one," Gemma remarked). Martino's mother had gone to town in Gianni's car to do something he couldn't explain, some errand, no doubt.

What Martino took care not to reveal was that he'd been walking up and down the main road for hours to make sure he didn't miss Giulia, and that's how he ran into the Leader. He'd tried to get away, but this time the other boy wasn't about to be surprised. He'd come up to him and grabbed him by the jacket collar, almost choking him, dragged him down the bank, stones hammering against Martino's sacrum, his lungs unable to keep pace with the galloping of his heart. At that moment, though, it all seemed worth it because his embarrassment could pass for the demeanor of a boxer, one who'd been honorably beaten. A few glances of silent admiration came from Giulia: rays of sun filtering through a closed shutter.

Luisa gave him a cup of Ovaltine to drink and treated his lip with ice and antiseptic cream.

Giulia went out to the kitchen garden and Martino, hesitant, lingered at the French doors, the external stairs, and then by the gate, finally reaching her where she stood amid the last yellow blooms of the Jerusalem artichoke.

"Let's go to the chapel," she suggested.

60

THE TEACHER ANSWERED the entryphone immediately and Lea said her name. There was quite a long pause, after which he repeated her name as if he couldn't believe his ears. That irked her—*Well, if I'm this easily annoyed I'm not so sure,* she thought.

"Am I disturbing you?"

"No, absolutely not. I didn't expect—third floor."

She found him waiting at the door when she got out of the lift. He no longer seemed taken aback, but neither did he seem ready to dispense with small talk and jump on her. He offered her coffee and *canestrelli*, daisy shortbread. They made broken conversation, both distracted by what they were about to do.

"There's an elephant in the room," she said.

"Well, yes. It's you."

"Thanks a lot."

And they kissed. She didn't know him and all his strangeness came out in that first kiss, but she was ready and waiting for it. He put too much passion into it, was uneasy and overdid it in an effort to get across how much he liked her. He held the nape of her neck in his large hand, moving his lips from her cheeks to her neck as if her lips had no boundaries or will of their own.

Someone rang the bell—not from outside, but from the inside landing.

"That'll be my neighbor. She sometimes brings me lunch on the weekend. I'll be right back." He pulled the door to and went to open up. She heard him speaking to a woman in a friendly voice, neither agitated nor hurried. He came back to show her an aluminium tray pearled with steam; inside were hot stuffed crepes.

"We might be hungry later," he said.

Lea stood up. "I'm not sure what's gotten into me, but maybe it's better if I go."

"Why?" Now he really was thrown.

"There are plenty of reasons."

"There weren't any when you got here."

"You're right. But I have to think about it."

"Did I say something?"

"No."

"Do something?"

"No, not at all. Maybe just the interruption. It gave me time to see myself from the outside."

"Are you okay?"

"Yes, yes, I'm fine. I'm sorry. I came here in a whirlwind and now I'm making a run for it."

"I was just getting used to the idea."

"Yeah." She picked up her handbag. "Am I presentable?"

"Absolutely."

"All right, then."

He went to the door with her and called the lift while she waited in his small, untidy hallway.

"Are you worried that the neighbors will see me?"

"No, I'm not even married."

"No, I guess you're not." She kissed him gently on his black beard and the desire to embrace him came back to her.

"Are you really sure?" he asked, a hand on her elbow.

"I'm sure. Sorry."

"Okay."

"I might come back, though."

"Whenever you want."

Back in the road, Lea looked up and saw not the teacher but the gray head of a woman, a bit past it, peeping out from behind the curtains on the second floor. She waved goodbye and the head disappeared.

61

GIULIA HAD FOUND A STICK and she was tapping it against the stones "because there are vipers, though they're probably already hibernating." She was agile and the tendons of her calves darted, tight cords under her skin. Martino had a hard time keeping up with her. Side by side at the little chapel, they met the fixed, vaguely bewildered look of the Madonna and Child.

"So why are they black?"

"Well, it's the Madonna of Oropa, who is actually a wooden statue. Have you ever been to the sanctuary?"

"No."

"It's up the mountain. Inside the church is the Black Madonna. I don't really know why they made her black, though. There's also an erratic boulder."

"Those rocks dragged by glaciers?"

"Yes, exactly! The Celts adored them. Until the nineteenth century, women who wanted children went to the church to bump their bums against the rock because they thought it would bring good luck. That's what my mother told me."

The conversation made Giulia turn red with embarrassment. "Come on! Let's keep going," she said hurriedly.

"Well no, no, really." Martino stopped her. "Why don't we go and see Maria's goats instead?"

"I don't like her. She kills everyone's animals."

"But you eat chicken and rabbit." Anxiety was making him unpleasant.

"They're already dead. I'd never kill with my own hands, that's for sure. Look, I want to go to the top. You don't have to come."

"No! Well, no, I'm not coming. Because of my asthma."

"Oh."

"I can't. I'm sorry." He was filled with shame. To safeguard his secret he had to pretend to be useless, someone who not only let himself get beaten up but couldn't even climb a hill.

"Okay, we'll see each other later," she decided.

"Giulia."

"What is it?"

"Do you want to see my room?"

"Sure. Wait for me there. I'll have someone show me where your house is. Actually up there is a place where deer sleep and I want to find it. I think you'd like it. Too bad about your asthma."

"Okay then. Bye," he said darkly, and he started going down, dragging his feet. If Giulia unearthed Silvia she would hate him forever. But maybe his things would escape her notice, at least at first. Well, surely not *The History of the West*. Damn it.

He heard the grass moving behind him and turned to see Giulia hurrying to reach him, her hair flying around her face. "I changed my mind."

They gave each other lopsided smiles out of shyness.

As they headed toward the village, Martino managed it so that his hand brushed Giulia's as if by chance, knuckle to knuckle. He felt like whistling.

Soon afterward, though, his bedroom with her in it seemed bare and full of the wrong things, at the mercy of who knows what: it was as if he himself were standing there in his underwear. He showed her his comic books and Giulia made a show of appreciating them, despite the fact that pistols, killers, and stormy seas were boy-things.

"He's good, this Hugo Pratt, but what an odd name," she commented.

"It is a pen name, and also I think his father was English."

It seemed she was only interested in the drawings. With her index finger she traced the figures as if learning how to redraw them. "Two lines, *bam, bam,*" she whispered. "But why does he make their foreheads stick out so much and their eyes so sunken, sort of like monkeys . . . When I draw, I like making rounded foreheads."

Martino felt hurt and he picked up on a little spitefulness. To him it was truly presumptuous to criticize Hugo Pratt's foreheads.

"Cherubs have rounded foreheads," he sneered.

"So what?"

He improvised, saying whatever came to mind. "So these are war stories! About pirates!"

"You're right," she admitted, catching him off guard. "It's clear that you have to adapt your style."

They didn't know what else to say to each other. Something stood between them and they didn't know how to get rid of it for good. So Martino alluded to the teacher once more, like someone who almost wants to be found out. *The tongue finds the tooth that hurts*: Lea was always saying that.

Seated on his bed feeling contrite, Giulia confessed something important: by now she had no more illusions. Silvia was dead. She didn't expect her to come home and was trying to accept it.

Martino didn't understand. He wanted her to go on hoping and tried to convince her to do so. The teacher was still alive, she must be for sure, and he continued in that vein, mulishly, until Giulia became angry.

"Stop it!"

"But I really believe it."

"You're just saying that for the sake of it, to be nice."

"No, that's not it."

"So you think someone can walk around for days and days without being found? Alone, with no money, no handbag? Didn't you hear that they found her bag with everything in it, even her wallet? What's she eating, according to you? Fried air?"

"Maybe someone . . ."

"Stop it!"

Her eyes looked so upset that he shut up in a hurry. She left without even saying goodbye.

62

There wasn't much left of the afternoon.

Martino stayed stock-still for a moment but hurriedly pulled himself together: in a frenzy, he collected water, bread, and an almost empty jar of jam and ran outside. Pain knocked once more at his injured lip and he shook with anger and frustration. On purpose, he thumped his schoolbag to the ground against the trees. He didn't even give Silvia time to ask about his bruise, and for the first time he spoke fearlessly and without deferring to her.

"They're looking for you along the river—Anselmo and Gianni and I don't know who else. I was with Giulia at the chapel and she wanted to come up and find the place where the roe deer sleep, right around here, but I convinced her not to. She got angry too. And before that I got beaten up by an older boy. My mother hasn't come back yet. You sit here quietly as if nothing matters to you."

"How long?"

"What?" Martino wrinkled his forehead.

"I don't know how long I've been here."

"I found you a week ago, I think. But you've been gone for longer."

The teacher's hair was crusty. She'd wrapped blankets around herself and held them against her chest with ashen hands. Her gaze, however, was clear, as if she'd just rinsed the blue of her eyes. She reached out and with her index finger touched the fabric of Martino's trousers near his knees.

"I'll come back. I promise you."

"You already said that once."

Silvia nodded.

"So, when?" he pressed her.

"Very soon."

"Now?"

"Not now, but very soon."

Martino was suspicious. "Do you still feel bad?" he asked.

"That girl, Giovanna. I really loved her."

"But thinking about people who've died and feeling sad about them is something that happens to everyone."

"Yes," she admitted.

"Giulia, for example, believes you're dead. But you're not. On the contrary, you are someone who's alive."

The teacher stopped talking and Martino wasn't sure how to interpret her silence. He tried to imagine what he would say to his mother in such a situation but couldn't. The more he thought about it, the more it seemed to him that it was about choosing between the living and the dead and which was more important. He was convinced that you had to look to the living and so, in the teacher's case, go back to them. But he couldn't have explained it because it was a feeling rather than a thought, and standing there, mulling it over, made him wish for a hot supper and a good sleep. He ended up saying goodbye, and went on his way.

63

IN THE EARLY DAYS of the search they'd called her name loudly, hoping to be heard, and urged the dogs on when they came back to rub damp noses against their palms. Now they let them roam loose. They didn't call out and they spoke as little as possible among themselves. Sandra was there, with sneakers on her feet and a woolen shawl around her shoulders. And Maria the Big Mouth, swallowing her saliva and holding her side but refusing to let anyone help her. Renzo was there, Bruno, Serafino, and everyone who'd been children and adolescents together, played hide-and-seek or pretended to fight beside the Quargnasca. Sister Annangela and Marilena completed the expedition: they arrived late in the Fiat Cinquecento; they'd been searching the village's disused cellars and abandoned houses for hours before on their own.

With her short legs, Sister Annangela had to go around trunks and bushes that Anselmo had stepped over or tromped down without even seeing them. A few steps from the water there was a cold smell of metal and anise, but here and there another scent of wax, wet fibers, and semolina pudding. Broken branches of elder exposed their white sap like the fragile bones of a bird and reawakened something in Marilena's memory: words dating back to stories she'd read with Silvia at boarding school. So when she recognized the lid of a coffin among the ferns, she thought she was hallucinating.

With her hand she signaled to Sister Annangela, but the other woman was unruffled. "I can't believe they're still turning up," she said. Marilena understood and calmed down: it was one of the coffins torn from the earth by a flood two years earlier, when apocalyptic rain had turned entire mountain slopes soupy with mud and detritus. The flood had wiped out bridges, and landslides had swept away stretches of woodland, cars, textile machinery, animals, people, and cemeteries.

"Do you think there might be a skeleton around here, too?" Marilena whispered.

"I have no idea. Look over there: I think that must be the clamp from a loom." Sister Annangela said a prayer and the two women moved on through the elders and bilberries, taking care to avoid the remains and rubbish they encountered, though it was difficult to tell them apart.

Anselmo and Gianni, both lanky, were almost walking as a pair. Gianni was a couple of years older, and there was a time when Anselmo had eyed him suspiciously because he saw how Silvia idolized him and because, during the war, he'd come at night with two companions and a Sten gun over his shoulder to take money from the partisans' trunk his grandfather kept hidden in the house. His grandfather actually thought well of Gianni, and Anselmo had ended up convincing himself that he really was half genius.

It was late and before long they'd have to use torches, but Anselmo didn't notice; he kept going, head down, irritated by the tenacious, triumphant vegetation that got in his eyes seemingly on purpose to make him stop. He ended up asking the others to spread out, while Gianni still trailed him.

"You see how the woods recover completely. Until a few years ago there were only meadows up here." Anselmo stopped to scan the landscape. "Silvia and I, though, we always went from around the Rivi hill."

He shook his head, and Gianni thought he could see tears. He was about to go up to him and put a hand on his back when they heard shouting behind them. They turned quickly, stomachs gnawed with tension.

It was Maria, who'd twisted her ankle badly and was sitting in the middle of some weeds sulking. "I can't put any weight on it. Go ahead. You can pick me up on your way back."

"No, we'll go back now," Anselmo chirped. Maria and Gianni looked at each other dumbfounded, but a minute later he swore in his usual loud voice and they felt heartened.

"What a fool I am, what a fool," Maria repeated while Sandra wrapped a handkerchief around her ankle.

They made a seat with their arms to carry her to the closest hamlet. She giggled to camouflage her pain and Anselmo and Gianni did the same to conceal the strain. Just for an instant, Anselmo imagined that he was carrying Silvia.

64

The lights were on in Martino's house and Lea was waiting for him. She'd put a parcel tied with red ribbon on the table and made a real fuss about his bruised lip, hugging and kissing him. She swore that the other boy would hear about it, the thug—he wouldn't get off easily. All the while Martino begged her not to do anything because these things were his business and his business alone.

The present was a big box of watercolors. Martino thought Giulia would be excited about them and he let himself get carried away too. In fact, he'd be able to take them to school and use them to make peace.

The next morning, Lea still hadn't exhausted her concern. She took him a cup of milk and biscuits and put his clothes on the radiator to warm.

"Listen, I've invited Agostino to lunch at ours," she told him as they got into Gianni's car. "I phoned his parents yesterday evening while you were asleep. Did I do the wrong thing?"

"No, no you didn't do anything wrong."

"Does the smell of smoke bother you? I feel like it's soaked into the seats."

"No, Mamma."

Lea rolled the window down. "There. Breathe in some more of that good air. It's like using your nebulizer."

The damp asphalt reflected the sky's pallor. Martino thought he could tell Agostino the truth about the teacher. After all, he lived somewhere else and didn't even know who she was. He'd also tell him about the wild boar and how he'd thrown a dead animal at an older boy and got in a fight over it. He sucked on his injured lip so he could taste the rusty flavor of dried blood.

"Leave your lip alone," Lea chided him, before adding, "It's a good thing we have the car. Gianni is really a good egg. Like Papa, you know."

Martino wasn't listening. He was mentally embroidering the tale he was going to tell Agostino.

They went past the big house by the fountain where Silvia had been born, if he'd understood properly, and the wall at the bend with the now familiar writing painted over in whitewash: GIMONDI IS BETTER THAN MERCKX. Above the hill hung huge, soft clouds, seemingly made of flannel. As they drove away from Bioglio and the woods, Martino realized that he was happy.

65

SILVIA MADE HER PREPARATIONS in the night, feeling her way. She put the canteen, folded blankets, and empty jar in a corner along with some leftover wrapping paper. Between the pages of *The History of the West* she slipped the heart-shaped leaf of a cyclamen, a fragment of mica, and a treecreeper's feather she'd picked up from the base of the beech tree.

She leaned against the doorway of the hut like a swimmer unable to decide whether or not to dip her big toe in cold water. It was a long way, and it would take hours.

Small, luminous discs gleamed in the dark: the eyes of a fox or a badger. She walked through the woods whenever she could, avoiding paths and the road. The plants breathed around her and every so often she stood back against a trunk, holding on to a knot and letting the sound of an animal in flight go by, another one hunting, something being plucked, a scrabbling just over her head. Near the edge of the woods, where the darkness was less dense, she recognized poisonous mushrooms and the venomous flowers of false saffron: a quick end had always been within reach if only she had wanted it.

Brushes of cardoon bordered the meadows, still wet and plunged in shadow. A few sleepy cows raised their muzzles to her, solemn and large; a red dappled cow extended its rubbery tongue toward the nettles growing beyond the cow guard.

Nettles, little nettles
Alone I passed you
Alone and raw, I ate you,

Silvia whispered, like Maid Maleen in the Grimms' fairy tale. She missed Giovanna's face and the combative expression—without reproach but also devoid of mercy—she'd worn when she appeared in the hut. It was a while now since she'd turned up.

The really difficult part was putting her feet on the asphalt and looking toward the hard, linear buildings. She closed her eyes to cross the bridge over the Cervo and inched her way along the cement railing, bit by bit . . . Her fingers were still sticky with resin and sooty mold.

The city was sleeping under a creamy mist when she stood outside Anselmo and Luisa's house at dawn. She swayed in her tiredness and gripped the door handle, her life stuck at an angle like a stripped screw that won't take hold and doesn't fit in its tracks as it should. Maybe she'd been worn away by the death of her mother, maybe before or perhaps later. *Oh well,* she said to herself, *that's how it is.*

The sound of the entryphone pulled everyone out of bed.

Author's Note

This is a work of imagination, but some of the events narrated are based on a true story that I began to reconstruct as a child, picking up scanty allusions and conversational fragments because it was a painful and delicate story, one not openly spoken about—at least not with me.

My grandfather's cousin, a teacher, never married and she had no children, yet she was an integral part of the family. She lived next to my grandparents in an adjoining house and ate lunch and supper with them. At the time, she was already retired and well loved by generations of former students. She was different from the other women who brought me up—my mother, grandmother, and great-grandmother—who were defined by having been mothers and married, divorced, or widowed. She may have been more alone, but in my eyes she also had more freedom. She didn't cook, didn't clean house, didn't do anything one expects of a woman. Added to that, she was extremely absent-minded and distracted, a character trait we have in common and that bound us together. I was also struck by the fact that she was an orphan who had spent years at a boarding school with nuns. She didn't speak much about the boarding school, where she had been very unhappy despite having made great friendships.

Already her story seemed to belong in a book. Characters in novels, especially those for children, are often orphans (Oliver Twist came to mind, Sophie in *The BFG* by Roald Dahl, Mowgli in *The Jungle Book*, Anne of Green Gables, Jane Eyre).

Eventually it became clear to me that something had happened to scar the teacher as an adult. She went missing for days, only to come back home almost dead of hunger and thirst, soaking wet from the rain, and absolutely filthy. Where had she been? No one knew for sure. Probably hidden in a church, having drunk holy water to survive. But why had she gone away? No one wanted to tell me. I found out later: one of her students, a girl of nearly twelve, had committed suicide by jumping into the river, and the teacher felt responsible because she had told the girl's family that she was often absent from school. Pain and a sense of guilt made her lose her mind.

The teacher never spoke about it with me and I never dared to ask. My father, however, remembered well the anguish of those days, the search and then her unexpected return: the doorbell ringing at dawn.

Her story did not stop calling to me after her death. At its heart is an undisputed event that resists the telling and remains unexplained and opaque: a young girl's suicide.

Before I wrote or imagined anything, I felt the need to reconstruct the facts, or rather, the version of the facts given at the time; attempts to decipher them; the behavior of those who had lived nearby or written about them. For this reason, I spoke to people who had witnessed the event and I combed through contemporary newspaper articles. Those texts helped me focus on what I wanted to say, how I wanted to say it, and why—they helped me to find, as it were, the truth that corresponds to the specific shape of the novel and has to do with the human condition, the hearing of voices that seem faint but continue to speak to us, regardless of how many years have passed since it all took place or how much has changed since then: language, school, education, economic and political conditions.

In various articles that appeared in the *Corriere Biellese* and the *Biellese*, the account alternates between expressions of alarm and attempts to explain or judge two events that elude comprehension. A girl commits suicide; her teacher disappears: "However, both facts plunge too deeply into the dark recesses of the human psyche," which remain impenetrable (this quote and the following quotes are literal, as is the one in Chapter 18).

The articles report such baffling details about the girl that using them in the novel would have made them seem artificial, and hopefully to some degree they are. For example: "After a lot of shouting, a sudden silence, and the mother goes to the sitting room which faces the millrace: M. M. is no longer there, but she's left her shoes on the window; the tragedy is announced in an enigmatic note on the table: *What are two shoes doing on the windowsill?*" Interpretation of the girl's act leads back to her premature adolescence and the desire for rebellion arising from it:

> Private expressions found in her diary allowed one to glimpse signs of early youth in a girl who had already

> matured physically beyond her peers. . . . Perhaps the reason for the girl's reckless reaction is hidden here; she already felt she was a woman because of a few furtive glances and some innocent approaches, and she was offended by what she considered an unfair reprimand. A reaction, however, for which no blame should go to the teacher: she alerted the parents; it was her express duty. After all, not everyone who gets told off for skipping lessons—even if harshly and with physical punishment—decides to put an end to their days.

The teacher is an enigma. She is described as a model instructor:

> She was what one calls an old-fashioned teacher: nothing but home and school. Her work was her world and distractions had no place in her life. It's true to say that she very often stayed at school during the break between morning and afternoon lessons, making do with a sandwich for lunch, or after hours to help students who needed special attention. She had been entrusted with that class precisely because she was known as someone with rare gifts of patience and affection who could extract the best results from "difficult" students.

The theory of a second suicide becomes increasingly persistent while simultaneously remaining unacceptable (there are interviews with friends and acquaintances while the family remains silent). In the meantime, the search is complicated by anonymous phone calls and false leads. The solution comes just when everyone is expecting to recover another body. But "the teacher's odyssey" remains a mystery, because the woman maintains that she remembers nothing. Or maybe she intends to say nothing.

The novel emerges from that lacuna and fills it with imagination.

There's a woman brought up by her grandparents and nuns who becomes a teacher thanks to her hatred of boarding school. Teaching becomes her mission, the center of her life. Though she has no children, she cares for generations of them and tries to be a good teacher (in contrast to the nuns), only to end up with a dead student. What disturbs the balance of her mind?

Just as in fairy tales, where it's often children who solve problems and relationships are inverted, the adult, the teacher, hides in the woods and a child takes care of her. Martino never existed, but he is a personification of all the children who were important to the real teacher. I am convinced that it's thanks to them, her fondness for them and her attachment to her role as a teacher, that she said yes to life once more and returned home.

I can add this: after months of convalescence, the real teacher went back to teaching. Today the village school bears her name.

Acknowledgments

I'd like to thank everyone who contributed to the editing and publication of this book, lending me their experience and intelligence: Chiara Valerio, Alice Fornasetti, Marzia Grillo, Claudio Panzavolta.

Thank you to Stefania Di Mella, Cristina De Stefano, Gabriela Jacomella, Maria Moschioni, and Marta Barone for reading, suggestions, and your affection. Giulia Caminito gave me important advice about naming places and describing them freely.

Thank you to Paola and Massimo, my parents, and Ermanno, my grandfather, who has a little bit of Anselmo in him.

Thank you to Maria, Francesco, and Irene.

Thank you to Tullio, more than ever, for everything he has done for the novel and for me.

A Note from the Translator

Approaching a text as rich and accomplished as Maddalena Vaglio Tanet's first novel is a daunting prospect. It is a work of fiction rather than a poem, yet Tanet is also acutely alive to poetry. The two poems of the epigraph, by Amelia Rosselli and Azzurra D'Agostino, brilliantly capture the mood of the novel, and poetry is woven throughout the book in the form of Silvia's hallucinatory reveries, exchanges between Gianni and Martino on John Donne and Gerard Manley Hopkins ('Glory be to god for dappled things/For skies of couple-colour as a brinded cow'), marching songs remembered from the war, verse quotations from fairy tales, and in the work of the Piedmontese poet Angelo Brofferio, whose dialect poems Silvia shares with her grateful student Giovanna. Nearly every chapter in *Dear Teacher* ends with a poetic observation, and the opening line of the novel is itself infused with a lilting rhythm.

Poetry is notoriously difficult to parse in one's own language, let alone someone else's. Slippery pronoun referents (often though not always intentional), subtle internal rhymes, idiosyncratic rhythms, and a personal lexicon are all part of a writer's *batterie de cuisine*. Added to that, Italian is a musical language whose beauty is enhanced through the insistent repetition of sounds and ideas in a way that English is not. On the contrary: from an early age, English speakers are taught to avoid repetition, to pare down their formal writing, clean it all up. So one of the greatest challenges of translating from the Italian—yet surprisingly one of the most enjoyable—is to find a way of anglicising these emphases and repetitions without sacrificing their intrinsic rhythm and beauty: to preserve the poetry inherent in the prose.

If poetry is a more or less obvious stumbling block, everyday diction in Italian is no less challenging to translate, since idioms in any foreign language must be learned and cannot simply be translated literally, even if doing so results in a string of constituent words that make a certain linguistic sense. In the gorgeous closing lines of Chapter 42:

> A family of roe deer are sitting on their haunches among the cyclamen in the small glade, but when one of them scents [Silvia's] presence
>
> and pricks up its ears, the others rise in unison and flee *pancia a terra* [as fast as they can].

A literal translation would render this phrase as 'flee, stomachs to the ground', which is confusing to say the least. The idiom, however, conveys the idea that the deer are running so fast that their bellies almost seem to touch the earth. None of the many optional idioms in English reflects the poetry of Tanet's writing about nature in the right way.

It is as important for a translator to capture voice and tone in a novel as it is for the author to establish them in the first place. In *Dear Teacher*, there are almost as many different voices as there are characters, and because Tanet makes ample use of free indirect style, there were numerous registers to reproduce, ranging from that of the curious, adventurous, and displaced ten-year-old boy, Martino, to those of the middle-aged curmudgeon Anselmo and the feverish visions of the starving teacher, Silvia. Given the setting in the 1970s, it was also important to consider the appropriateness of the vocabulary used in the translation alongside the inevitable issues of class and gender, all of which have an impact on speech.

Translation is a multilayered task which starts with basic semantics. But in the end, it is really about listening. A translator needs a good ear, not just for the music of the original text but for that of her own, as well: for the respective rhythms of each, since they often differ wildly, and both must make their own kind of poetry. I hope that this English version of *Dear Teacher* succeeds in channelling something of the power and beauty of the Italian original.

Here ends Maddalena Vaglio Tanet's
Dear Teacher.

The first edition of this book was printed
and bound at Lakeside Book Company
in Crawfordsville, Indiana in April 2025.

A NOTE ON THE TYPE

The text of this novel was set in Baskerville MT Pro, a typeface published by Monotype and based off the Baskerville font family designed by John Baskerville (1706–1775). An internationally recognized writing master and printer, Baskerville's innovative style and high standards for printing gained him many admirers and imitators. The Baskerville font is considered emblematic of eighteenth-century neoclassicism. Highly legible and incredibly dignified, the typeface is particularly suited for books and advertising materials.

HARPERVIA

An imprint dedicated to publishing international voices,
offering readers a chance to encounter other lives and other
points of view via the language of the imagination.